Ghost

Mystika

THE MANY RHODES WE TRAVEL LLC

Also by

To explore more of the Supernatural Chronicles World:
Click GHOST for Amazon purchases!
Click HELL for Amazon Purchases!
Click HYBRID for Amazon Purchases
Click MAGICIAN for Amazon Purchases

Use this link or QR Code for lots of extras!
https://linktr.ee/mystikaauthor

Dedication

This book is dedicated to my mom, my husband, son, and to anyone who has a dream that they never give up on.

CONTENT WARNING: The main characters deal with graphic depictions of sexual assault, physical abuse, domestic violence, knife injuries, and rape. If this may be triggering for you, please put your mental health first and proceed with caution or skip this story completely

Contents

Chapter 1

Nicholas: July 12th, 1861

"Good morning, children," I said as I stepped into our one-room, dilapidated schoolhouse. Teaching children, no matter their economic status, was very important to me.

"Good morning, Schoolmaster Nicholas," the group of children responded. Most of the children were yawning. They woke at sunrise to assist their parents on the farm, milking cows and feeding the other animals. Soon, many of the children would assist in the harvest season while we take a break from school. The other children in class were orphans, raised by the church.

"Please pull out your New England Primer textbook," I instructed while pulling out mine. "Thomas, you may start."

"A. In Adam's fall, we sinned all. B. Thy life to mend, this book attend," he stuttered through the first page of letters. He had improved immensely. Slightly older than the other children, his parents had died from illness on their way over to America. The class included children from the ages of seven to twelve. Children up to age fifteen had attended in prior years.

The morning classes flew by after we finished reading. Writing and arithmetic were not my favorite subjects to teach, but I knew they were important for our society. I scurried home, famished for my Emily's cooking. I enjoyed lunch with my wife.

We didn't live far from the school. It took ten minutes to walk there. Cows and horses grazed in many of the fields I passed. Emily had wanted me to take my horse, but he was not acting his normal self. The midday break lasted ninety minutes, allowing for a meal and a brief moment with Emily before resuming.

As I entered town, walking quickly along the cobblestone street, I spotted Charles up ahead, delivering mail. He was the local mailman and known to everyone. As I approached, he waved, and I returned the gesture.

"Afternoon, Nicholas," Charles greeted me with a friendly smile, shielding his eyes from the sun that was behind him. "Beautiful day."

"Indeed, it is." I tilted my head toward the clear blue sky. "One of those days that makes you forget all your troubles."

"What kind of troubles would a man like you have?" Charles asked, his brow furrowed.

"I... I didn't mean I did, but all men have some form of trouble." I said, trying to understand the reasoning for his words. Before I could inquire further, one of my pupils ran up, holding a worn-out ball.

"Can you play catch with me?" he asked, excitement in his voice.

Charles hesitated, stealing a quick glance at me before shaking his head. "I don't play with kids. Besides, I have work to finish," Charles said, faster than I could react. The boy spun towards me.

"Okay, I was asking Mr. Nicholas!" the child stated with the bluntness only a child possessed. A brief flicker of hurt crossed Charles's face, masked by a forced chuckle.

"Now, that wasn't very nice, Timothy," I chided. "Mr. Charles is busy. We should speak kind to others."

Charles shrugged, giving a brief dismissive laugh. "It's alright, Nicholas. It did not hurt my feelings. I've never cared for playing with silly children."

With a forced casualness, I couldn't shake the feeling the boy's words stung more than Charles let on. Timothy gazed at me, and I mustered a smile, patting his shoulder.

"Perhaps later, after school. I am headed home to eat." The boy nodded and ran off. Charles and I continued our journey together.

As we strolled along, the conversation resumed. "Did you hear about the animal attacks near the edge of town?" Charles asked, breaking the silence.

I rotated my shoulders to face him, taken aback. "Animal attacks? No, I hadn't heard. What happened?"

Charles shifted his mailbag on his shoulder. "I heard it was a bear. They found a couple of sheep mauled in Mr. Thompson's pasture. Shocking."

The thought unsettled me. "Bear? I didn't think they traveled this way. Rarely do they come close to civilization."

"Rare, indeed," Charles agreed, nodding. "But the tracks were unmistakable, they say. Some folks are even talking about starting a hunting expedition to track it down."

I felt torn between intrigue and concern. "That sounds dangerous. Bears are unpredictable, especially if they're hungry or threatened."

Charles rubbed his chin. "True. But the farmers are concerned for their horses and pigs. Again, something you would not have a trouble for."

I looked at Charles through a side glare. His lips were up in a bit of a smirk. "What is so funny?"

"Everyone in this town says how noble and nice you are, but sometimes your words disagree with them." Charles stated. We walked in silence, my mind twirling on his words. I never meant to say anything off putting, yet Charles had taken every word I said to heart. *Charles has known me for so long,* I thought, *wait, how long has he known me? It has been at least...* My memory went cloudy at that moment. I couldn't remember what I had been just thinking about.

As we approached my house, Emily came out onto the porch, her face lighting up my heart. I loved that she loved my childhood home and filled it with love just like my mother had. A whiff of yeast tantalized my nose. Emily must have been making her delicious bread. My stomach growled with every step I took. Last year when she baked this bread, she paired it with a mouth-watering stew. We ate stew most weeks, but this recipe she cooked sparingly. It was her mother's famous recipe. She would not tell me the secret ingredient. On her deathbed, her mother swore she would never tell another living soul, not even me! Her resilience in keeping the secret was admirable.

"Nicholas, your timing is perfect," she called out. Then, noticing Charles, she added, "Hello, Charles. Lovely afternoon, isn't it?"

Charles showed a brief lapse, his usual easygoing demeanor wavering. "G-good afternoon, Emily," he stammered, fidgeting. He raised his head during the tense pause, meeting her stare. "God knows how to create a beautiful world," he said, his voice uneven.

Although uncomfortable, I understood why Charles found himself captivated by Emily's blue stare. However, Charles never acted this way with any of the other females in town. He has been this way with Emily for... *why can't I remember how long I've known him for?* I asked myself. My hand went to my head as it went fuzzy again.

Emily, ever gracious, did not seem to notice his stuttering. "Would you join us for lunch? There is plenty," she offered.

Charles hesitated, then nodded. "I-I could, if it's no trouble," he said, a shy smile on his lips.

"Not at all," Emily said in her welcoming tone. "Come in, both of you."

Emily walked inside, and Charles's hand collided with my chest forcing me to halt in place. "See, how could a man have any troubles when he comes home to a woman as beautiful as she?"

Charles said with a bitterness to the words, then he entered the house. I understood why he thought her beautiful, but his words towards me felt bitter. I did agree with him. I was the luckiest man.

Inside, Emily arranged three plates on the table. She walked over to the huge black pot and stirred the contents, causing the air to become filled with the aroma of herbs. I walked over to her, hugged her from behind, my whole-body tingling with the joy of having her in my arms.

"Oh, Nicholas," Emily laughed. "I missed you so."

"How was your shift at the hospital?" I asked. Her lips turned into a frown.

"Let us not talk about work. We have a guest," her attention now on Charles. As we sat down, Charles appeared to relax, despite still stealing the occasional glance at Emily.

Emily shared stories of her garden, and Charles narrated a few amusing anecdotes from his postal route. The ambiance was light until Charles lifted a spoonful of potatoes. He paused before taking a bite. Almost immediately, his face contorted, and he spit the remaining food into his bowl.

Everyone's attention shifted to him in surprise. "There must be garlic and– "he started, wiping his mouth with a napkin.

"Vervain. Both great seasonings from my mother's secret stew," she said, her smirk widening as she met Charles's eyes– as though she was confirming a suspicion he hadn't voiced aloud.

I couldn't hide my surprise. "You've got quite the palate, Charles. I've been trying to figure out those ingredients for years."

Charles pushed the bowl aside, not enjoying the discovery. He leaned back in his chair, one arm draping casually over the backrest as if reclaiming space that wasn't his. "Well, it's not to my taste," he muttered, his voice carrying a mix of discomfort and mild annoyance. "You know, Emily, you should be careful with those seasonings. Back in my old town, they used to accuse women who handled vervain of being witches."

His gaze lingered on Emily a beat too long before flicking to me, a silent challenge in the subtle arch of his brow. Then, as if wanting to pivot the conversation, he refocused on me.

"I hear they're forming a hunting party for the bear," Charles mentioned, tearing off a piece of bread. He tore it slowly, methodically, each motion precise. "Men with wildlife knowledge are needed. Nicholas, you're adept with literature, especially about animals. Maybe you should join them."

There was a faint smirk on his lips, the kind that darted me to refuse.

Surprised by the suggestion but intrigued, I took a big gulp of my water. "Me? I suppose I remember a bit about animal behavior from my readings. It could be useful."

Emily's expression shifted to concern. "Nicholas, I feel that's not a smart idea," she said, her voice tinged with worry. "We lack knowledge of the situation. The animals simply survive as they must. They're not mindless killers."

Charles raised an eyebrow, interested in the budding debate. "True, Emily," he conceded, his tone smooth, but his eyes sharp. "But if this predator is a threat, shouldn't we protect the community?"

I nodded, agreeing with Charles. "He's right. While I have sympathy, it's already attacked livestock. It may attack our family and friends."

Emily sighed, setting down her fork. "But there might be a reason. Perhaps the poor dear is lost or injured, or a different predator has disturbed its home. Jumping straight to hunting seems... drastic."

I frowned, not understanding her hesitation. Charles's hand brushed his glass, but he didn't drink; he just traced a slow circle along the rim, the faint hum oddly commanding the silence. Emily and Charles stared at each other, never blinking. Why, I wondered. "We cannot sit back and hope it goes away, Emily."

She looked down at her plate, upset. "I know that, Nicholas," she mumbled. "I think you should use your brain for other conclusions before hunting. Let's consider hiring an expert in wildlife and pest control."

The tension in the room was palpable. Charles broke it with a low chuckle– not mocking, but heavy enough to reclaim everyone's attention. "Whatever happens, I'm sure they will make the right decision. It's important to have different perspectives. Right, Nicky boy?" Charles said, emphasizing on the nickname, leaning forward just slightly, the corners of his mouth curling in satisfaction when I nodded.

The rest of the conversation was lighter. As Charles prepared to depart, he turned toward me with a pensive look. "Nicholas, you've always been good with your book smarts, but don't forget to listen. There is a lot of wisdom around you," he said, glancing at Emily. "Some of us," he added softly. "Learn best through humility."

He stepped closer– too close– and laid a firm hand on my shoulder. The pressure was friendly in appearance but unyielding underneath. "You're a lucky man to have someone who thinks so deeply about things. You don't deserve her, you know?" He chuckled, though there was a hint of seriousness in his tone. His penetrating stare met mine, and I felt an unusual weight in my limbs. I desired to step away, but my body defied me. It was as if something was holding me in place, an invisible force beyond my control.

Then the sensation faded. I could move again, and I managed a smile, feeling a twinge of discomfort. "I'm grateful for her daily," I said, trying to lighten the mood. There was an awkward silence, the air thick with unspoken tension.

Charles's expression softened. Although he nodded, I could still sense an undercurrent of something deeper in his words. He stood up, straightening his jacket, his posture precise and practiced, as though reclaiming the last word without saying anything more. He gave Emily a polite nod before heading to the door. But as Charles left, his words lingered in my mind, leaving me to ponder whether I understood and appreciated my wife's perspective. His comment seemed more than a passing remark.

"I want to talk about us," Emily stated. She had been occupied the last few weeks working extra shifts with doctors since the Union Army had been enforcing new regulations and the consent threat of Confederate raids.

At the beginning of the year, she had a miscarriage when a patient kicked her in the stomach while getting their arm reset.

I can still see the pain in her eyes even though her beautiful lips say she doesn't blame herself. She pulled me over to the table.

"I think it worked this time." She said, her lips arching up in a smile.

"Are you certain, my love? It's only been a week." I said, my eyes staring deep into hers. She nodded.

Emily placed her hand on my cheek. "I and our future child are lucky to have you."

We exchanged smiles briefly. Though she claimed she was ready to attempt once more, I worried about her well-being. Perhaps selfish, but I would rather be childless than see her hurting. I brought her forehead down to my lips.

"I'm the lucky one." I said, kissing her lips. "I need to return to my class soon."

"Of course. How are they doing?" she asked. I loved that she was always so curious about my students. She rejoiced in their triumphs and shared their sorrows.

"They are doing very well. Learning so quickly," I said. Emily went to the stove, pulled out the bread, and cut it. I noticed an intricate symbol etched into the handle of the knife, something I had never seen before. She wrapped them in a cloth and brought it over to me.

"For the stroll to school. Give you energy to continue your day." She handed me the bread with a small vial of clear liquid. "A special tonic to keep you strong," she said. I kissed her, holding gently to the back of her neck so she wouldn't pull away. Her lips were soft. Even as we separated, our focus remained on each other. I could not bring myself to leave, especially with her looking so poised to strike. I bowed to her and turned to leave, regretting my exit with every step.

Chapter 2

Nicholas

Walking to school, I pondered how Emily always sensed my need for comfort or encouragement. Perhaps she could read my mind. Or maybe she could sense my feelings. I chuckled at the thought. My Emily, always understanding, knows what to say and do. Perhaps it was her loving nature, but sometimes it gave the impression of something more.

Walking to the school appeared ordinary. Birds were chirping. The sun was high in the sky. Horses fed on the grass and hay in the fields. A faint thunder caught my attention. The thunder grew louder, uninterrupted. I saw dust rising from the hills in front of me. Within a moment, I recognized the sound of horses' hooves, not thunder. The soldiers rode their horses at a swift pace. I jumped closer to the fence of the nearby farm to avoid being trampled. Dust kicked up in the air from the hooves pounding on the dirt. I covered my eyes with my arms until the horses passed and I continued my journey.

I walked on, vaguely observing the dust still rising from the ground. As it swirled into the air, it turned a grayish black.

This wasn't dust. It was smoke!

"Oh no," I yelled, running as fast as my thin legs could carry me. Flames were licking the sides of the doors, and thick black smoke obscured the windows. As children arrived behind me, their screams at the sight of the devastation echoed in my ears. Charles arrived when I did, his presence was both surprising and welcomed.

"Schoolmaster Nicholas, help," a pupil coughed as he knocked in desperation at the window. I almost didn't see him through the darkness. My breath caught in my throat as I realized the severity of the situation. I dashed to grab a bucket and filled it with water. Charles was already there, rounding up the children.

"Sarah, run and fetch help. Everyone else, line up so we can expedite this bucket to the well," I commanded. Sarah ran off as the others listened to my demands. We had to run between each other, but Charles's agility astounded me. He moved with incredible speed, aiding in the transportation of the water to and fro. Charles wasted no time barking orders as more adults arrived, his voice carrying authority that silenced even the loudest cries. For a moment, I found myself following *his* direction instead of the other way around.

When I reached for a bucket, Charles brushed past me, his shoulder hitting mine harder than needed– firm, deliberate.

"You handle the children," he said curtly, his tone leaving little room for argument.

Once the flames were under control, I rushed into the building, navigating through the smoldering wreckage. Charles was right behind me, tossing desks and debris aside as if they weighed nothing. "Careful," I warned, but he didn't even glance my way. His movements were too forceful, too precise. My jaw dropped in awe at his incredible strength, but I could not dwell on it. My focus was on finding Timothy.

When I tried to lift a beam, Charles pushed me aside, one hand gripping my shoulder. "You'll slow us down," he said sharply before yanking the beam free as though it were made of straw.

"Timothy. Timothy, where are you?" I called out, trying to suppress the urge to cough. Near the window, I spotted a small foot sticking out from under a desk. Panic surged through me as I threw the desk and debris off him. I searched for a pulse at his neck, but there was none.

"Timothy," I sobbed, resting my forehead on his chest. My failure crushed me. Who possesses the cruelty of ending a child's existence? I trembled with a mixture of grief and rage.

****

The day passed in a haze. The image of Timothy's lifeless body haunted me, even when I tried to shut it out. Why hadn't I been faster? It was my fault. Had I taken the horse, as Emily suggested, or had not left for lunch at all, I would have been there.

"Do not blame yourself, Nicholas," Emily whispered, lifting my chin. Her words brought me to the present moment. I was home, though I had no recollection of leaving the school. Her arms hugged me throughout the night, but sleep evaded me. I feared the nightmares that awaited.

Before dawn, silently, I dressed. My wooden chair across from the bed was the perfect placement to watch Emily sleep. I smoked my pipe, the tranquility broken only by the murmur of voices outside. Curious, I glanced at Emily, still asleep, then made my way to the door.

Outside, my neighbors had gathered, their voices a mix of fury and grief. Frederick's shout cut through the noise. "We cannot let those soldiers get away with this," he roared, his brows furrowed and nostrils flaring with rage.

"Good morrow, gentlemen. What is the matter?" I asked, though I already had an inkling. I noticed that Charles was amongst the group. He seemed to be around a lot.

"We are going to war with those blubbering soldiers for what they did to that child," Jeremy declared, his jaw tight, his eyes burning with righteous anger.

"Nicholas, we both seen what happened. We should be the face of this town. You are the brains, and I'm the muscle."

The memory of Timothy's lifeless body flashed in my mind–his laughter silenced, his future stolen. The ache that had lingered for days erupted into something fierce and consuming. I could no longer bear to stand by while others suffered the same fate.

"I agree," I said, my voice trembling with conviction. "A fight is needed."

As my neighbors continued their talk of enlistment and vengeance, a knot of fear and determination twisted my chest. I slipped back into the house, the air inside heavy with the scent of the morning fire. Emily was awake, sitting at the edge of our bed, her hands clasped tightly in her lap.

"What's happening out there?" she asked, her tone already laced with worry.

"I must join the war," I said, my resolve firm. "I need to fight for Timothy– for what they've done to him, and to all of us."

Emily's eyes welled with tears. "Nicholas," she whispered, "what about our future?"

I frowned, uncertain what she meant. Then she took my hand and guided it gently to her stomach. Her fingers trembled as she said, "I have not bled this month. I..." she stopped as a faint creak came from the porch, Through the thin curtains, I caught sight of a shadow moving. I hurried to the window, but no one was there. "I think I'm with child again."

I brought my head in from the window as the world seemed to still around us. My anger gave way to a flood of emotion– hope, fear, love– all at once. I pulled her into my arms, pressing my forehead against hers. "Emily... this is wonderful news," I murmured. "Our family will live on. That's all the more reason I have to fight. I can't let this world take another innocent from us."

Tears slid down her cheeks as she shook her head. "Promise me you will come back to us, Nicholas. Promise me you won't let the war take you too."

I cupped her face in my hands, brushing my thumb over her wet cheek. "I promise," I said softly, though a part of me feared it was a promise I might not be able to keep. "I will come back to you both."

I enlisted the morning after the meeting– July 14th, 1861– a date I would never forget. The ink on my enlistment papers had barely dried when the reality of my choice began to sink in. Now, a week later, July 22nd, would be another day I would never forget. The morning sun cast a warm glow over the fields as I stood outside, dressed in my new Union uniform. The fabric still felt stiff and unfamiliar against my skin. The weight of my decision pressed heavier than the rifle on my shoulder, but deep down, I knew it was the right thing to do. As I adjusted my cap, the sound of soft footsteps approached from behind.

Emily hurried to me, her face flushed and swollen from crying. When she reached me, she held me. In my ear, she whispered, "I don't want you to leave, but I understand," she said, her sentence faltering. My heart shattered a little more.

I wrapped my arms around her, holding her close. Smelling her hair, the warmth of her body against mine—it was all so familiar, so comforting. Yet, the reality of our situation loomed large. "I don't want to leave you either," I murmured. I wiped a tear from her cheek. "But I must do this. For you and our child."

She nodded, understanding but not lacking pain. Then she reached into her pocket and pulled out a small carved knife. The blade gleamed in the morning light, and I noticed the strange markings etched along its surface. Symbols or runes, but their meaning escaped me.

Emily pressed the knife into my hand. "Take this," she said, wiping tears from her face. "It's been in my family for generations. My mother bestowed it upon me when I married you, and I'm lending it to you. For protection."

The cool metal of the hilt pressed against my skin as I examined it. Although the markings eluded me, I felt comfort. Slipping it onto my belt, I turned to her. "Thank you, my love." I said, softly. "I will keep it safe until I can return it to you." I leaned down and kissed her, pouring all my love and passion into that moment. Her lips engulfed mine in a comforting warmth, making everything else fade.

But reality returned all too soon. With a deep breath, I gazed at her once more. "I will return," I vowed.

Each step to the waiting carriage was burdensome, but I understood I had to bear it. As I climbed in, I glanced over to see Emily's hand on her stomach, watching me leave. I offered her a reassuring smile, hoping it would bring her some comfort.

As the carriage started moving, I clutched the gift at my side, feeling the weight of both the metal and the vow I made. I was heading into uncertain and dangerous times, but I also carried a piece of Emily with me. That thought granted me strength as I ventured into uncharted territory. Determined to return to my family, regardless of any obstacles.

It took us a full day's journey to reach the training grounds, as our small band of volunteers had to travel to a neighboring town where the larger companies gathered to drill. The roads were dusty, the air thick with summer heat, and conversation among the men quieted as we drew closer to our destination. By the time we neared the encampment, a knot of apprehension had formed in my stomach. When we arrived, I stepped down from the carriage and took in the sight before me– rows of tents stretching across the field and soldiers moving with practiced precision. They were rugged, broad-shouldered men, their confidence evident in every stride. In comparison, I felt slight and untested, my frame lacking the hardened strength theirs carried with ease.

Among them, I spotted Charles. He stood tall and broad-shouldered, blending in with the other men. I experienced a pang of envy and insecurity. The men eyed me with curiosity, some with amusement. I was out of my depth.

The next morning, we had our first regular workout session. I joined a group of men lifting heavy sandbags. My arms quivered under the strain, and I could lift half of what they were managing with ease. Laughter erupted in every direction, and I felt my face flush with embarrassment. The men snickered and exchanged glances, their words biting.

"Looks like we got ourselves a new weakling," one of them jeered, loud enough for everyone to hear. Another chimed in, "Hope you don't need to carry anything heavy in battle, or you'll be in trouble!"

I looked at Charles, seeking some support. He met my gaze and offered a noncommittal shrug offering a slow smirk instead.

"Don't strain yourself, schoolmaster," Charles said under his breath as he walked past. His hand brushed my arm– a friendly gesture at first, but his grip tightened just enough to make me flinch. "Wouldn't want you breaking something before going to the war."

Instinctively, I reached into my pocket and squeezed the knife Emily had given me. It reminded me of her and of the life we had built. It gave me a comforting sense of connection, a reminder of my purpose.

Days passed, and the routine continued. Each morning, we gathered for grueling workouts, and I pushed myself harder. The others lifted weights, ran drills, and sparred with ease, while I struggled to keep up. My muscles ached, but I refused to give up. I focused on each movement, determined to prove that I could keep up, that I belonged. The laughter and taunts became a background noise I tried to ignore.

The officers frequently commended Charles during this time, praising his strength and precision during sparring. "That's fine work, Charles," one sergeant remarked after a round. "If more men fought like you, this war would already be over." The other men clapped him on the back, and though he tried to play it off with a smile, I could see the pride gleaming in his eyes.

On our third week of drills, I completed every exercise without faltering. My heart pounded with exertion, but there was a new feeling there— pride. I had done it. I had pushed through the pain and self-doubt and had come out stronger. As I paused to breathe, I felt accomplished. This time, the officer called out for everyone to hear. "Blackstone, you've shown the most improvement out of the entire company." For once, the laughter didn't follow. Instead, I caught Charles watching me, his jaw tight and his expression unreadable.

The men, however, continued their banter. They laughed, unimpressed by my progress. I scanned their faces, looking for a sign of acknowledgement, but found none. It stung, but I told myself it wasn't significant. I knew what I had achieved.

As we finished up, Charles walked over and clapped me on the shoulder. It wasn't a hearty gesture, more of an obligatory acknowledgement. "Not bad," he said, his tone neutral. Then he joined the guys as they headed off.

I caught up, determined to keep pushing forward, regardless of what challenges lay ahead.

On a sunny afternoon in the fourth week of training, we assembled for a strategy exercise as our commanding officer laid out a scenario on a large map spread across a makeshift table. The scenario involved defending a strategic position against an advancing enemy force. We were to discuss and decide on the best defensive strategies. The group began tossing out ideas, most suggesting brute force methods akin to building barricades and holding the line with sheer numbers.

As I listened, I realized they were missing a key opportunity. I cleared my throat, hesitant but unwavering. "Sir, if I may," I began, stepping forward.

"Let the officers handle this, Nicholas," Charles said lazily from his post. "We don't want to get too clever for our own good."

I hesitated as the other men laughed, but the officer nodded for me to continue, forcing Charles to step back. His jaw twitched, the only sign of irritation he allowed himself. The men became quiet; their attention focused on me. I could feel their skepticism, but I pressed on. "Instead of focusing on fortifications, we could use the terrain to our advantage. There's a narrow pass here that the enemy would have to funnel through. If we position sharpshooters along these ridges and create a bottleneck, we could reduce their numbers before they reach our primary defenses."

The room was quiet as they considered my suggestion. The commanding officer leaned over the map, nodding. "Good point," he said, now respecting me more. "Using the terrain effectively can be as crucial as having strong defenses."

Encouraged, I pushed on, "And if we dig a few shallow trenches here and here," I indicated two spots on the map, "we can protect our men from artillery fire while still allowing them to return fire efficiently. It doesn't require much labor, just some planning."

Charles, who had been leaning against a post, straightened and studied the map, his interest apparent despite his silence. The rest exchanged looks, some agreement with subtle gestures. For the first time, they regarded me differently, not merely as the weakest among them.

The commanding officer smiled. "Okay, let's implement these ideas. Nicholas, you will oversee placement of the sharpshooters and digging the trenches."

As we executed the plan, I felt confident. The team followed my directions, and as we worked, I noticed a shift in their attitude. They asked questions, sought my input, and even shared their own suggestions. Despite lingering skepticism, they respected my value.

By the end of the day, we organized the defenses, and the officer conducted a mock drill to test our preparations. Exactly as I had predicted, we successfully stalled the simulated enemy force at the pass. Our "casualties" were minimal, and the commanding officer praised our efforts, highlighting strategy and planning.

As the men dispersed, the commanding officer pulled me aside. "Nicholas, I've been watching you closely. You've made remarkable progress, and your quick thinking today proved invaluable. If you continue at this pace, I'll be recommending you for an officer's position when training concludes in two weeks." I stood straighter, stunned. "Thank you, sir," said quietly, still absorbing the weight of his words. He nodded and moved on, leaving me both humbled and proud.

As I strolled to my tent, Charles joined me, his steps slow and deliberate. He moved closer until I could feel the heat of him beside me. When I tried to step back, his hand landed on my shoulder, heavy, unmoving. "I genuinely didn't think you would make it in here," he remarked.

Shocked, I stared at his incredibly serious expression. "Then why did you mention that I should join?"

Charles hesitated, his jaw locking. "I am uncertain," he replied, his tone edged with frustration. "But I think you are selfish, leaving Emily. Like I said at your house, Emily deserves better."

The criticism was painful, and I held back a defensive retort. Charles turned and took a few steps before he halted and lowered his head. There was a moment of deep hush before I reached him, unsure of what to expect.

"I am a predator. I get what I want," he expressed. His delivery low and foreboding.

A chill ran down my spine. "What is it you want?" I inquired, struggling to keep my composure despite the unease creeping into my chest.

Charles's eyes flickered with an emotion I couldn't decipher. "Everything you left at home," his voice barely above a whisper.

I stood there, bewildered. Unusual intensity filled his gaze, as if wrestling with internal turmoil. He both loathed and envied me, a puzzling mix of disdain and longing. When he spoke about Emily, it was as though he longed for what he thought he could never attain, resenting me for having it.

Before I could respond, Charles rotated and sauntered off, leaving me standing there, thoughts racing through my head. His unsettling words resounded in my ears. I watched him disappear into the shadows of the camp.

Chapter 3

Nicholas: March 10th, 1862: 6 months later

"Charles, watch out," I yelled, pulling him forcefully into the trench where he landed on his stomach. I crouched down beside him in the smoky, sulfur-filled air, my heart pounding as we waited for the chaos to subside.

"My hero," Charles coughed out, his tone dripping with sarcasm even in that life-and-death situation. He sat up, leaning against the dirt wall, wincing as he held his injured arm. I held his musket towards him. Charles gritted his teeth, but his eyes blazed with determination as he shook his head. "I can't, they shot my arm."

"No, this is your duty," I insisted, handing him his musket. Charles stared at me, not budging. I hesitated for a moment, grappling with the reality of what I was about to do.

"You've got this," he urged, his voice firm.

I nodded as I steadied myself. I still wasn't comfortable with killing, even after our six weeks of training and our six months of battling, but Charles trusted me in that moment. I raised the musket, my hands steady despite the adrenaline coursing through my veins. I looked through the sight, aligning my target.

I held my breath as I took aim, slowly releasing air as I tightened my finger on the trigger. The shot rang out as the recoil jolted through my body. Dust rose, momentarily obscuring my view as the enemy fell.

The battlefield seemed eerily quiet after the shot; the only sound was the faint rustling of soldiers emerging cautiously from their fortifications.

"Are we safe?" Charles asked, his voice cutting through the silence.

"I think so," I replied, my eyes scanning the surroundings, alert for any new threats.

"We need a surgeon over here!" a voice yelled to the right of me. A young recruit ran over to him. His hands shook while removing the shirt of our comrade. The recruit was barely a man.

"We need to set up a field hospital. Quickly, over here!" another man yelled. He pointed at a red door to the local school. I blinked quickly, as I recognized the building. We were a few towns over from my home. We had been traveling so much this last year, I hadn't realized where we were.

"Everyone needs to come inside here for triage. After we do all we can for them, move them to the second floor for recovery."

"If the surgeon cannot save them?"

"Then we'll stash them in the basement," the man commanded, straightening up amidst the chaos. His face smudged with ash, he shifted from soldier to commander, aware that seconds were ticking away for our wounded comrades.

"We need a blockhouse. Williams where are you?" he bellowed, striding towards First Lieutenant Williams.

I felt disoriented, unsure where to lend a hand. Hastening to Charles's side, he was busy aiding other soldiers, hauling the injured into the school. I grasped the hand of the next suffering comrade. Strained grunts escaped my lips as I pulled.

"Move, Nicholas!" Charles took my place. Rubbing my arms, I felt inadequate compared to robust men like him. Although I had been getting stronger, my body would never be their size. Above the turmoil, I heard a woman's cry. Racing up the stairs, I saw a young woman with a child sobbing in the street. I hurried to her side.

"Are you hurt?" The woman shook her head, tears streaming down her face. Her son lay limp in her arms. Gently laying him down, I recalled a London physician's book advising on saving lives by repositioning and applying chest pressure. Sweat beaded on my brow as I pressed on his chest, praying for signs of life. The mother wept as I worked, surrounded by anxious soldiers. A local woman comforted her.

"Breathe!" I accidentally shouted, feeling like someone else inhabited my body. With one final push on the boy's chest, I leaned close, whispering, "Please, God. Spare him."

Expecting to see the boy stir, I felt Charles's hand on my shoulder. He shook his head. The mother wailed. Helping her to her feet, I attempted to console her as the crowd dispersed. Moments later, the mother gasped. "Anthony!"

I turned to see Charles kneeling beside the boy, one hand cradling his head, the other pressed against his chest. His face was bent close, too close, murmuring something I couldn't hear.

Then, to my astonishment, the child drew a sharp breath. His eyelids fluttered. The crowd around us froze. Slowly, the boy sat up, dazed, and looked around as though waking from a dream. His mother cried out in joy, gathering him into her arms.

"How–?" I began, but Charles rose to his feet before I could finish, his expression unreadable. "You did it, Nicholas," he said, clapping me on the shoulder hard enough to make me stumble. "Your prayers worked."

As the mother thanked me between sobs, the boy turned and hugged my waist. That's when I noticed the streak of red along his neck. Frowning, I wiped it away with my sleeve. Two faint puncture marks dotted his skin.

"Must've been shrapnel," Charles said quickly, his tone light, but his eyes darted to the marks before meeting mine. "Come, let's get them to the surgeon."

Applause broke out among the soldiers, shattering the eerie stillness that had fallen. I forced a smile, though my mind was still on those tiny wounds and the way Charles had looked when the boy gasped back to life.

Soldiers parted, and there was my commander, clapping.

"Nicholas," he greeted with a smile. "Once you've tended to these civilians, find me."

With that, he walked to a nearby tent for officers. I watched until he disappeared inside, feeling a familiar weight on my leg. My gaze returned to the child, fear behind his smile.

I waved my hand over a set of chairs for the mother and child to sit. I walked over to a nearby nurse whose smile reminded me of Emily's. I missed her so much. I pointed to the child and his mother.

"Please watch over them for a while. They've been through a lot." She nodded her head and squatted down next to the little boy. I watched as my mind wandered for a few moments before I walked towards the front door.

Helping more wounded into the school, I knew I had to see my commander. Unsure if I faced trouble for aiding civilians or practicing medicine without being a surgeon, I was in no haste to see him. I couldn't let a child die. If roles were reversed, I'd pray for help for my own child.

Stepping out of the school cautiously, I caught the officers' canvas tent, hastily pitched nearby. Inside, the dim light of the oil lamps illuminated their faces, as my commander engaged in discussion with fellow leaders.

"What brings you here, Blackstone?" a gruff voice called out from one of the leaders.

"Commander Lewis sent me to find him," I stuttered. The commander turned from his table, eyes narrowing at me.

"Nicholas. Yes, come," he beckoned.

"Yes, sir."

"Nicholas Blackstone– did you know a Paul Revere, by any chance?" I nodded. "Good. Paul spoke highly of you, and I see why."

Walking to a wooden table with a map upon it, he gestured for me to join. I glanced at the unfamiliar markings on the map, trying to understand. He gripped my shoulder.

"I have a special task. Take this map to Commanding General Grant. It is of the utmost importance." He rolled up the map and handed it to me.

"I will ride fast. Where is he located?"

"Appomattox Court House. This needs to stay quiet. No one else can accompany you. If you are captured, the other side will win the war with this map."

"What is on the map, sir?" I asked shyly. I felt if my life was on the line, I should know what I was protecting. Commander Lewis pulled me away from the others.

"It's the markings of our hidden weapons." He quietly said. I felt a chill as I wondered what kind of weapons, but I didn't pry. "Take one of the horses," he said. I nodded slightly and walked out of the tent.

My mind raced as I exited. My most important task would be traveling on the easiest terrain for the horse, not to tire it. Suddenly, words echoed in my mind from Commander Lewis. *If you are captured, the other side will win the war with this map.*

Emily's face popped in my mind. Her and I did not see things eye to eye when I left. With this task being so dangerous, I need to see her one last time before I go further from home. This is the closest I've been since I left for training over six months ago. Besides, I've missed so much of her pregnancy. Getting to glimpse at her belly will make me so happy.

A chill went down my back, and my neck twisted around. No one was there, but my body felt an unease like someone was watching me.

Grabbing oats for the horse, I stuffed the feed bag. I saddled the horse and headed down the road.

The cadence of hooves on the dirt echoed to the beat of my heart. The life I cherished was getting closer with each stride. Emily's face emerged in front of me. Emily's smile was a beacon of hope in the darkness of war. Laying in the cold muddy trenches, I swore I could hear her voice urging me to stay strong and return home safely to her. Laughing, I realized how much I missed the children playing loudly in the classroom. Plenty of times I would yell for them to quiet down. Now I yearned for those laughs over the howls of pain echoing across the battlefield.

It hadn't all been chaotic, though. Moments like today—riding beneath the vast expanse of the sky, the crisp air filling my lungs—brought peace. The quietness of the countryside brought time to reflect on my journey from scholar to soldier, from the safety of academia to the realities of the battlefield.

Thinking of Emily patiently awaiting my return, I nudged my horse onward. These last six months of war had changed me. I was a man of action now. Yet deep down, I remained the scholar who believed in the pursuit of knowledge, even in the midst of war's chaos. I wondered how her pregnancy was going. She had to be showing by now.

"Emily," I yelled, approaching our small farmhouse. The sight of the apple trees I helped my father plant filled me with a mix of relief and longing.

I dismounted my weary horse, and I filled my hand with oats to feed him. I glanced back at the house. It was dark, and Emily had not run to me yet. It was unlike her to take this long to come outside. It was not late enough for her to be sleeping. Worry gnawed at the edges of my thoughts.

"Emily," I shouted again, as my footsteps pounded on the wooden porch. Shoving the door open, a sinking feeling settled in the pit of my stomach.

The warmth was replaced with an unsettling stillness. Emily was not in sight. Where could she be?

A faint sound, carried on the evening breeze, reached my ears. A high-pitched scream. I turned around, exiting the front door. My heart pounded as I scanned the familiar surroundings. The screams filled the air again; this time I could tell it was from the woods.

Fear gripped me as I entered the woods. Could it be Emily? The screams became louder with each branch that snagged my uniform. I did not care, though; I was desperate to find my wife.

Stopping, I looked up as I saw a huge cave. I had forgotten about this place. Emily and I used to sneak in here to meet before we wed. It was the only place we ever had time for ourselves away from our families. Memories rushed back of our first kiss. Now tainted by the fear that held in my heart.

Although my mind told me to turn and run, I took a deep breath and stepped into the cave. The air was damp and heavy with the scent of sulfur. Torches lined the jagged walls

– something I didn't recall from our youth. Their flickering light stretched shadows across the stone, warping them into monstrous shapes that moved as I did.

I moved cautiously, weaving between boulders slick with moisture. The sound of shuffling echoed ahead– slow, deliberate movements that made my pulse quicken. A faint crunch broke beneath my boot. When I looked down, my stomach turned– Emily's amulet. She never took it off.

My hand trembled as I braced against a boulder and peered around it.

Emily stood in the center of the cavern, her body illuminated by the nearest torch. Her hair hung loose around her shoulders, and both hands rested on her rounded stomach. Even through the loose folds of her dress, the curve of her pregnancy was unmistakable. She looked healthy, but her expression was wrong. Vacant. Still.

"Emily," I whispered.

She didn't move. Her eyes were locked on something just beyond the light.

A shape moved beside her – tall, familiar. When the torchlight caught his face, my breath stopped. Charles. The sight hit me like a musket ball. For a heartbeat, I couldn't breathe. Tingles ran down my spine. His uniform was torn, streaked with dried mud and something darker, and his face – though familiar – looked sharper, colder, as if carved from stone.

It didn't make sense. Charles should be with our comrades.

"Charles?" My voice cracked as I stepped out from behind the boulder. "How– how are you here?"

He turned his head slowly toward me, the movement deliberate, almost feline. His eyes caught the torchlight, gleaming with something unnatural. Without saying a word, he shifted his stance, placing himself directly between me and Emily. My instinct screamed danger.

A chill ran through me. The man I once knew was gone.

"Why is it," Charles began, packing a slow circle toward my left, "you always get what you want?" His tone was calm but laced with poison.

I moved instinctively, stepping in front of Emily. My arm stretched protectively behind me, as her shallow breathing brushed against the back of my neck.

Charles smirked, never breaking eye contact. "And what do you think you can do to me?" he asked, the corners of his mouth curling upward.

The torchlight glinted against his teeth– too sharp, too white.

Before I could respond, Charles moved. One instant he was standing ten feet away, and in the next he blurred across the space, slamming into me with inhuman speed. As I crashed into the ground, dust exploded around me. Emily stayed frozen, her eyes glassy, her hands still cradling her stomach as if she couldn't feel a thing.

Charles's hand clamped around my throat, squeezing hard enough to steal the air from my lungs.

"Now I will take everything away from you," he hissed. He dragged me closer to Emily. His lips met hers, slow and possessive. She didn't fight back – didn't even blink. Her stillness was more terrifying than the act itself. His grip slightly loosened. It felt like an eternity before their lips unlocked, and tears rolled down my cheeks. Emily's eyes stayed glassed over, her face never moving. It's like she was in a trance. Charles then lowered his face toward her belly and rubbed it. Panic surged through me, and I felt the ground around me until my hand wrapped around a jagged rock. I swung wildly, the edge cutting across his cheek.

Charles recoiled, then slowly straightened, touching the blood on his face as if amused. His grin returned– wider this time, and much crueler.

"Now you've pissed me off," he said softly, "I was going to let you die an easier death. Now you'll be my toy."

He lunged again, his full weight slamming me back against a massive boulder. Pain shot through my ribs– a cracking sound echoing through the cave.

Was that the stone breaking... or me?

"Nicholas!" Emily's voice trembled, full of terror.

I turned toward her just as Charles drove the jagged rock into my chest. A white-hot pain tore through me, and I looked down to see the stone slick with my blood, buried deep in my heart.

Emily ran to me, tears streaming down her face, her hands pressing desperately against the wound. Her swollen belly brushed against my arm as she knelt beside me.

"My love, you are so beautiful," I managed, my voice breaking. I rested my hand against her belly. "You're going to be an amazing mother to our child. I am so blessed to have been loved by you."

"Hush, Nicholas. You'll be okay," she whispered, trying to steady the rock in place. Her hands were warm– so painfully alive.

"Run," I told her, my strength fading fast. "I love you."

Charles seized her by the shoulder and tossed her to the ground. Then he hoisted me up by my throat again. My vision blurred, but I saw Emily reaching for her amulet on the dirt floor. She clasped it around her neck and whispered something I couldn't hear.

Light exploded around her as the amulet in her hand flared to life, glowing with an otherworldly brilliance that filled the space. I stretched my arm toward her, desperate not to lose her again. For a moment, I thought I'd grasp nothing but air, but then–our fingers brushed, connected, and a rush of warmth coursed through me. My knees buckled as if the ground had been ripped away, and I collapsed into her waiting arms. Her face swam above me, eyes shining with both sorrow and resolve. She whispered something that only a fragment reached me: "Charles... and Nicholas... intertwined..." The words tangled in my fading consciousness, and then the world slipped into darkness.

$$Chapter\ 4$$

Avery: April 10ᵗʰ, 2024

"Ok, Mrs. Jones. You are free to leave," the doctor said, followed by the nurse who had stayed by my side all night. I signed the discharge papers, my arm throbbing with each movement. Despite the nurse's concern, I had no choice but to drive myself. I needed to be far away from *him*.

I slid into the driver's seat, wincing at the pain in my arm. My car chimed for gas, and I prayed it would make it to the next gas station.

Thankfully, it did, and I grabbed some cash and snacks, determined to reach my soon-to-be-home without stopping again. At this pace, I would be at my aunt's home by 5pm tonight.

It had been ten years since I'd last been to my aunt's house, and the backroads all blurred together. I didn't trust my memory, so the GPS became my lifeline.

"In 300 feet, your destination will be on the right," my GPS stated. The sun shone in my eyes. I could barely see the road. "You have arrived."

I pulled up under an old grey archway. In rusted iron above the arch, it read *Blackstone*. I never really understood why they named houses back in the 1800s. A squealing noise screamed at me.

"Next on my list of things to fix: my brakes." My eyes widened as I saw the house. The light blue paint was chipping away. There was moss growing on the side of the house, dropping over the wide front porch. I had my work cut out for me, but it was all mine. No one was going to tell me how to take care of it. No one was going to tell me I owed them anything. It might not have been the greatest-looking place, but it was mine.

A white Chevrolet Corvette pulled in behind me. I closed my eyes for a second and breathed in and out slowly, doing the 4 counts like my psychologist taught me. My whole body tightened when a door slammed. Before I could see who it was, someone knocked on the window. I squealed as I glanced over to see a woman in a business suit, with long black hair that was perfectly straight. I smiled at her as I lowered my window.

"I am so sorry for scaring you, darling. My name is Rebecca. I am the estate lawyer. I was trying to get here before you, but life. Ya know," she talked quickly.

"It's okay. I was just admiring the house and you startled me. It is a bit bigger than I remembered."

"When was the last time you were here?" Rebecca asked.

"Oh gosh, I guess like ten years. My aunt and husband did not get along at all."

"Well, why don't we get ya out of the car and look around your new home," she said excitedly, extending the house key to me.

"That would be lovely. A refresher of the house is needed." I accepted the key from Rebecca and turned off my car.

Rebecca was talking about the history of the home from the 1800s, but I wasn't fully listening. This was the first time I'd lived alone in over ten years. I missed the friends I made in New York.

The bushes and shrubbery wrapping around the porch made for perfect privacy. However, it was also the perfect hiding place for *him*. I knew he was in jail, but that wouldn't last forever.

"Please be careful on these steps," Rebecca started to say. Pain engulfed the top of my foot, but I caught my balance. "As I was saying, some of the steps need replacing. Your aunt was very sick towards the end and did not keep up with much of the maintenance."

The key glided into the lock a lot easier than I had imagined. I twisted the doorknob, but the door didn't budge. I looked back at Rebecca, hoping she knew some secret way to open the door. She was too busy typing on her phone. I used my shoulder to push all my weight into the door. It rushed open, and I fell to the ground. My head pounded.

"You're accident-prone, aren't you, dear? Are you sure living on your own is safe? I bet we could find you a few roommates. You have enough space for at least two more families!" Rebecca stared at me as if I had grown multiple heads. I couldn't believe she wasn't even trying to help me up. I brushed off my yoga pants when I could raise myself. I found a scrape on my elbow.

"No, I'll be fine. I have ideas for what I'll be doing with each of the rooms."

"Great," Rebecca exclaimed. "Well, this is the entranceway. The black and white marble tiles are from the original owners. I know it doesn't look impressive now, but a little water and a mop will shine it right back up! You also have these two beautiful staircases. It's like something right out of a storybook!" Rebecca explained quickly. It made my head spin. She looked at her phone while she walked away.

"If ya follow me, you can see the spacious living room. The fireplace is *my* favorite part of this room," she said, placing her hand on her chest, as if that really helped me understand it was hers. I was ready for Rebecca to leave. I was ready to start my new life.

"You know a lot about my aunt's home," I stated.

Rebecca looked at the ceiling and then back at me, a smile beaming on her face. "I love this home. My mom and your aunt were friends. I came up here for a few different events growing up. When your aunt started to get sick, my mom told me. I knew I wanted to help her, and you, when the time came."

"I really wish I had been here more for her," I said, crossing my arms. I turned my face away from her so she didn't see the tears falling from my eyes. Rebecca placed her arm on my shoulder and smiled at me.

After a few seconds of silence, she asked, "Do you have a moving truck coming later today?"

"No, everything I own fits in my car."

"Well, luckily for you the house comes all furnished. Plus, our little town loves old and historical things so we have a plethora of antique shops!"

Rebecca looked back at her phone and started typing away. She hurriedly walked into the next room. I followed her to the next room. My mouth slightly dropped, gazing at the gorgeous sight of kitchen cabinets galore. The island in the middle was big enough for workspace for several people and dining at the same time. The kitchen wasn't shiny, but with some TLC, it would be. I would have room for multiple friends. Well, once I got them.

"So, this obviously is the kitchen. It has plenty of cabinet space for all your, well, future pots and pans. There's so much space you could bring in a whole catering crew!"

Rebecca watched me as I was taking in the kitchen. I thought something was wrong. It had been the longest her eyes had been off her phone.

"As much as I can see you're in awe of this room, we need to move faster if I'm gonna have time to show ya the whole house. It's huge!"

Rebecca rushed through the rest of the first floor, basement, and backyard. I liked the fact that it was going quicker. The stairs led to a long dark hallway. There was a chill that went down my spine. I felt cold all of a sudden.

"Is the AC on?" I rubbed my hands together.

"I don't believe so."

I rubbed my bare arms as we moved down the hall, peeking into each of the bedrooms. I hadn't been in this house for nearly ten years, and though it was still familiar, everything felt... off. The furniture was different, the wallpaper newer, yet the air carried that same heavy stillness I remember as a kid.

A prickle crawled up my spine. It felt like someone was watching me.

I knew my anxiety was probably just playing tricks on me. He should still be in jail, and we were in different states. There was no way he could've found me this quickly. Still, the unease clung to me like static.

Rebecca kept glancing at me from the corner of her eye.

"What?" I finally asked.

Rebecca sighed. "I was told I didn't have to disclose this, but you seem like a nice enough person. I feel I should."

"Spill it already."

"Well," she said, lowering her voice a little, "apparently there was a woman killed here. It was years after the Civil War. She was married to the local Civil War hero, Nicholas Blackstone. People don't like to talk about Emily Blackstone."

"That's awful. Why don't they talk about her?"

Rebecca shrugged. "From what I've heard, she was involved in some kind of black magic. Whatever it was, it wasn't something polite people liked to mention."

Great, just what I needed. A house that had a death in it. My luck I would have a ghost haunt me. I thought to myself. But then again maybe it wouldn't be a bad thing. I'm not oppose to helping a spirit pass on as long as they don't try to hurt me.

We stepped into another bedroom. The air felt heavier here, colder, though Rebecca didn't seem to notice. A shiver ran down my spine as I exhaled and saw my breath drift into the air like fog.

"How are you not freezing?" I asked, rubbing my arms.

She only smiled faintly. "You get used to it," Rebecca said, her tone too casual for how icy the room felt. Then she gestured toward the stairs.

"So, what will you be doing for work?" she asked while we walked back downstairs.

"Eh, I really hadn't thought that far ahead yet."

"Really? A girl of spontaneity," she said, her eyes narrowing playfully at me. I let out a loud and quick laugh. Rebecca blinked, clearly startled by the outburst.

"Sorry," I said, rubbing the back of my neck. "I wasn't trying to laugh that loud."

She chuckled, waving it off. "No, it's fine! Girl, trust me, I am *always* being told I'm loud. Ya don't have me beat."

We both laughed again, the tension easing as we stepped out the back door onto a huge wooden deck.

"What type of work have you done in the past?"

"Oh, I was a reporter for the *New York Times*. I was there for about five years."

"How come you left? Were you threatened by the mob or something?" she asked, half-joking but half-serious.

"No," I said with a small laugh. "No mobsters in New York for a very long time. I don't think I ever met a mobster in my life."

"Huh. Guess the movies lied to me," she said with a sheepish smile. "Anyway, I know the owner of *The Yeller Newspaper*. Let me know if you're interested."

"Oh wow, I'm interested."

"Awesome! I will set ya both up! She used to be a big town girl too. I don't know much about her backstory though. I used to try, but she always changed the subject." Rebecca started typing away on her cell phone. I looked out past the yard. There was a beautiful lake between me and all the neighbors. A slight wind almost drowned out the chime of her cell phone.

"Ok, my friend said she could interview you Friday the 12th, if you are up for it?" I turned to look at Rebecca.

"Are you kidding?" I asked, shocked. My head spun as reality kicked in that my aunt had passed, I was moving into her home, and now I might be getting a new job! I was excited and nervous all at the same time. Rebecca slowly shook her head.

"Once people get hired at this paper, they hardly ever leave. You just happened to come at the right time. Someone just retired," Rebecca said. I gave her a huge hug and smiled.

"Yes, I would love a chance to interview! I'm sorry, I was just shocked it happened so quickly."

"It's ok," Rebecca said, typing away on her phone. I turned toward the water watching the sunlight ripple across its glassy surface. The only sound between us was the gentle tapping of her fingers against the screen.

"Ok, I think we've been through every room inside and out," I said, forcing my gaze away from the shimmering view.

"Yes, we did," she replied with a laugh. "That was a lot faster than I thought it would be.

We both fell silent again, our attention on the lake. The air was calm, and the scene almost too peaceful to leave.

"I really think you will enjoy living here. You have an aura around you like your aunt. I think you will fit in here perfectly!" I looked over at her and smiled. The gentle wind pushed her hair back. Rebecca never took her eyes off the lake. "Well, I will leave you to settle in."

I waved goodbye as her car pulled away. A breath of relief escaped my lips. I hadn't even noticed I was holding it.

I leaned against the closed door after I locked it. I had forgotten how exhausting people could be. It had been over ten years since I was allowed to be around other people without him.

"I'm home," I said aloud to myself. Confidence and fear tangled inside me. I was so happy to be free of my old life, yet terrified it might find me again. And what was I thinking when I said yes to the interview? All my articles would have my name on them. Maybe I could be a ghostwriter. Write under a false name. My brain was thinking too far ahead. I only had control over what I could control at that moment. Nothing else.

I looked around. Sunbeams were shining through the windows, casting light over familiar furniture and old keepsakes. Relief washed over me—my aunt's things were still here. Right now, I needed to unload the car. I missed my stuff, but I had to grab only what I could carry. He could be getting out of jail by now.

I needed to make sure he didn't find me.

Chapter 5

Nicholas

My head pounded. Attempting to open my eyes was proving difficult. My hands slid against hard pebbles as I tried to sit up. The musty scent of the cave shocked my senses as I looked around. I raised my hand, holding a jagged piece of rock stained with blood. A chill ran down my spine—not just from the cold air, but from an overwhelming sense of familiarity.

I blinked into the darkness. *If only I had a light*, I thought.

At that very moment, a faint glow flickered to life. A nearby lantern–One I hadn't noticed before–slowly brightened until a steady flame illuminated the cave. I froze, my breath catching. "How..." The lantern's wick burned without oil, the flame unnaturally steady. I hesitated before lifting it, its heat strangely muted against my skin.

Gray rocks stretched in every direction, their surfaces slick with moisture. The air was damp, each breath bringing a sharp, icy sting to my lungs. Shadows danced across ancient carvings worn smooth by time.

A circle of boulders lay in the middle of the walkway, with ash still lingering in the center. I brushed some of the ashes away, revealing a Bible. As I moved the lantern closer, I inhaled some of the dust and ash, which caused me to cough. I grabbed the book, and a piece of paper fell out, floating to the ground. I bent to pick it up.

Memories flooded back—playing on these very rocks as a child, laughing and chasing my friends through the dark passages. We would hide in the nooks and crannies, pretending the cave was our fortress. The cold never bothered us then, our young bodies fueled by excitement and adventure. But now, the chill seeped into my bones, a reminder of how much had changed.

The cave seemed smaller now, the once expansive cavern closing in around me. The stalactites overhead dripped steadily, each drop echoing through the silence. I remembered the times we would dare each other to stand beneath them, the icy water sending shivers down our spines.

I shivered now, pulling my coat tighter around me. The familiar ache of the cold brought a strange comfort, grounding me in the present. I unfolded the paper, reading the words written in my love's handwriting:

Dear Nicholas:

I am sorry, my love, that I am not there to greet you. I know you have questions. Let me try to answer some. While you were dying in my arms, I tied your being to Charles. After months of trying to bring you back, I knew that my magic didn't work because I am not the strongest witch to defeat Charles. Although, I did try. You must find the strongest witch and help her stop Charles at all costs. I love you, Nicholas. Never question that.

Emily

A wave of confusion washed over me as I read the letter. My thoughts spun, trying to piece together what it meant. Tied my being to Charles? The words made no sense. What did that even mean? I rubbed my temples, the pounding in my head growing worse. The walls of the cave seemed to close in on me, and I knew I needed to get out.

As I stumbled toward the cave's entrance, light from the outside illuminated the rock in front of me for a brief second.

The forest outside felt... wrong. The air was crisp but heavy, unnaturally still. My footsteps made no sound, though I could see the leaves shifting beneath them. A chill rippled through me as I glanced down—no shadow stretched across the ground. "Strange moonlight," I muttered, forcing my mind to reason with the impossible. Emily would know what was happening. She always knew.

The sight of my house in the distance filled me with relief. But as I grew closer, my relief faltered. The blue paint glimmered in a way I didn't remember, smoother—newer. The windows had thin black frames instead of wood, and odd metallic tubes jutted from the side of the house, humming faintly. The sound was constant, low, and steady.

"What manner of witchcraft is that?" I murmured, watching droplets of water fall from the metallic tubes.

I climbed the steps, heart aching at every creak of the old boards. "I've only been gone less than a year…" I whispered to the porch beneath my feet. When I reached for the doorknob, my hand slid right through it. The sensation wasn't pain–just emptiness, like pushing through fog. I jerked my hand back, breathing hard. Then, bracing myself, I tried again My hand passed through the wood, tingling. Panic clawed at my chest. "What does this mean?"

I forced myself through the door. The house was exactly as I remembered–yet something was off. The lamps glowed without flame, their light soft and white. Strange boxes hummed quietly in the corners. The air smelled faintly of flowers and metal.

A woman's voice echoed from upstairs. My heart leapt. "Emily," I called, bounding up the steps. With each step up the creaking staircase, my anticipation grew. My heart ached with the hope of seeing Emily again. I couldn't wait to press her lips against mine and to rub her belly with our first child inside.

As I reached the top, I saw two women standing in the hallway. Disappointment washed over me when I realized neither of them was Emily. *What kind of respectable woman wears pants instead of a dress?* I thought to myself. Emily had always worn the most beautiful dresses. She would go to a special seamstress to make her gowns fit perfectly. I was beyond lucky to have a woman like my love.

I moved closer, listening to their conversation about the house. "Who are you?" I asked, but they didn't even glance in my direction. Frustration bubbled inside me as I repeated my question, louder this time. Still, they ignored me. One of the women kept rubbing her arms, shivering slightly whenever I got closer. "Is the AC on?" she asked, a hint of confusion in her voice.

"What is AC?" I muttered aloud, watching the other woman shake her head.

"I don't believe so."

Frustration welled inside me. "Please, can't you hear me?" I implored, stepping in front of her, but she looked straight through me as if I didn't exist. "Why won't you answer me?" My voice wavered with desperation. I waved my hands, trying to get their attention, but they continued their conversation, oblivious to my presence.

The chill she felt seemed to increase the closer I got, and her discomfort was evident. "What is going on here?" I muttered to myself, growing more agitated.

"Why won't you see me? Hear me?" I shouted, my voice echoing in the otherwise quiet house. Then, before I could move, she walked forward. I thought our bodies were going to collide, but the sensation was indescribable. Every nerve lit up as cold as death, and for a heartbeat I felt her pulse inside me, her fear, her warmth. And then—emptiness again. I stumbled backward, gasping. My mind reeled. *What... what am I?*

I looked into the face of the cold woman. There was something about her—some similarities to Emily. Her cheekbones, the shape of her eyes—they reminded me of my wife. Despite my sadness, I couldn't help but notice her beauty, which made me feel guilty. How could I think another woman was beautiful when my heart still belonged to Emily? And she is carrying my child.

As they continued to talk, I strained to listen.

"I was told I didn't have to disclose this, but you seem like a nice enough person. I feel I should." The other woman said with a sigh.

"Spill it already!" The cold woman said.

"Well, apparently there was a woman killed here. It was years after the Civil War. She was married to the local Civil War hero, Nicholas Blackstone. People don't like to talk about Emily Blackstone."

A surge of anger and sadness overwhelmed me. "No! That's not true!" I yelled, my voice echoing through the house. The women didn't hear me, but I followed them back downstairs, my emotions in turmoil. As I descended, I started to notice changes in the house. There were no flowers. Emily had always kept flowers in the house, their fragrance filling every room.

"Emily!" I shouted, searching every corner of the house. "Where are you?"

I moved from room to room, growing more desperate with each step. The house was both familiar and foreign. One of the women left, her absence like a puncture in my already fragile reality. Then, the cold woman began to bring boxes of things into the house, each thud of the boxes against the floor sending jolts of resentment through me.

"I'm home," she said with a huge grin. I huffed in annoyance. How dare she say this is her home? I didn't even know her! She wasn't even wearing proper attire for a woman.

"Excuse me! You must be confused. This is my home, not yours!" I pointed at her in reprimand. The woman looked around the house, even looking in my direction. Was she purposely ignoring me? She's wearing pants—there's a possibility she could be this disrespectful. She looked down, realizing the boxes had gotten dirt on her. She shook her head and wiped the dirt onto the floor. I had never been so flabbergasted in my life! I angrily walked over toward her, shaking my finger at her.

"You, madam, should know better than to wipe dirt in someone else's home! How dare you!" The woman ignored me once again and picked up the three boxes she had dropped earlier. I could feel my anger rising inside of me more and more.

The woman started to walk in my direction. There was no way she couldn't see me now. Another cold chill ran from the top of my head to the bottom of my feet as the woman walked straight through me! This feeling was too odd for me. I started to walk backward, trying to understand what was going on. The woman walked into the next room. I suddenly felt myself going backward from tripping over something. I was even more confused as I saw half my body was outside on my front porch while the other side was still inside my living room. My brain went blank. I didn't know what I should be thinking or feeling at this moment. I was walking through things. That woman walked through me. She couldn't see or hear me, for that matter! What the hell? Where is Emily? I just want to hold her in my arms! I want to feel my wife's soft lips on mine. My eyes burned with determination to find her. I picked myself up. With confidence and a sense of purpose, I walked over to the woman and cleared my throat.

"Ma'am, I need you to tell me what is going on," I said. I tried to get her attention by placing my hand on her shoulder. She spun around and walked through me again.

"YOU NEED TO STOP THAT!" I yelled with fury. I walked into the kitchen to calm myself down. I tried to control my breathing. I closed my eyes. I had flashes of Emily with Charles standing next to her, blood dripping from his mouth. Rage and confusion collided. I needed to hit something. I balled up my fist and slammed it hard into the table– and it connected. The impact was real, solid, the sound booming through the kitchen. For one brief second, I felt alive.

The woman came running, looking around. "Hello? Anyone there?"

I stood inches from her, trembling. "I am," I whispered, my voice breaking. "I am here."

But she couldn't hear me.

As I laid my head down on the hard, cold floor, my heart and mind started to fill with more doubt and loneliness than I had ever felt. I closed my eyes, trying to think of better times. I could hear the birds chirping a happy tune. A soft-checkered blanket lay beneath me. My legs tingled as Emily ran her fingers slowly and lightly over them. Her hair tickled my nose as the wind blew it in my face. Then the laughter of a young boy brought tears to my eyes as he dived on my stomach. It was the perfect day.

The creaking of the steps brought me to my current reality. I went to the stairs to follow the woman.

I watched as the she walked into mine and Emily's room. The memories of the last night Emily and I had made love flooded back—her laughter, her touch. The pain was almost physical, a knife twisting in my gut.

She started placing items inside Emily's old dressers. I clenched my fists, anger simmering beneath the surface. This was our space, our memories, and now *she* was invading it.

She went into the bathroom, and I followed. Her wrist twisted on a silver knob, and I watched as a steady stream of water flowed from the strange silver spout. "What witchery is this?" I whispered, eyes wide. She didn't need a bucket or a pump to bring water to her. The marvel of it almost made me forget my pain. "You wield strange magic, lady."

Water filled her hands, and she wet her face. When she looked up, a bruise on her eye became obvious. My anger shifted, morphing into a deep, aching sympathy. Without thinking, I reached out, my hand passing through her cheek. I felt a pang of sorrow for her. Her beautiful blue eyes, so striking, now marred by pain.

The woman smiled at herself in the mirror, "Hi, I am Avery Jones. It is nice to meet you," she said, repeating herself with different smiles and different pitches in her voice. Her lips, so mesmerizing, reminded me painfully of Emily. The woman started to put some cream around her eye.

"Avery. That is your name. It is beautiful," I whispered, feeling an inexplicable connection.

"I wish I knew who hurt you," I whispered into her ear, a deep sense of protectiveness welling up inside me. "I do not understand why, but I feel a connection to you."

As she placed a night garment on and laid in the bed, I felt a strange mix of emotions. A part of me was angry at the intrusion into my life, but another part of me was inexplicably drawn to her, wanting to shield her from any more pain.

"Emily," I murmured, my voice a mere whisper in the silence of the house, "where are you?"

Exhaustion began to creep in, my energy waning. I exited the room and went downstairs into a dark and quiet living room. The couch looked inviting, a small semblance of comfort amidst the chaos.

I laid down, my body sinking into the cushions. My eyes grew heavy, and despite the turmoil in my mind, sleep took over. The last thing I remembered was calling out for Emily one more time before darkness enveloped me.

Chapter 6

Avery

The next two days went by quickly. I stayed in the house cleaning all the dust from the furniture and opened the closed rooms my aunt hadn't used in a while. This was a huge house for just her.

I looked in the bathroom mirror, checking for any evidence of caked concealer around my eye. I had woken up early from a nightmare of the last beating Richard gave me. So, I had plenty of time before my interview.

As I drove my car, the radio played breaking news.

"Breaking news. The sheriff's office was called this morning. A group of hikers found a body lying in a ditch in Randolph Park. This will make the fourth death this week, all out-of-towners. The type of animal responsible for the attacks has not been identified yet by the coroner's office. A bystander said that the victim's face was mauled. The sheriff's department is on the lookout for dangerous animals that may be responsible. Curfew is now in effect at 7 p.m. Now, back to our music."

"Another mauling? This is not New York," I muttered to myself.

Arriving at the office, which looked more like a house, I felt nervous but hopeful. As I approached the door, a simple question popped into my head, and I said it before thinking twice. "Do I knock or just walk in?"

"You just enter. Despite the look, it's not a residence," a male voice chimed in behind me. I turned to see a tall man with short dark hair. His half-smile showed me he was joking.

"Thanks. I am Avery Jones." I extended my hand. He glanced down, then extended his.

"My name is Charles Smith. Nice to meet you. I need to get back to work, but nice to meet you," Charles said, entering the building. I could hear all the women saying hi to him.

I entered the foyer, then walked down the short hall to an opening on the left side. A woman was typing away. She glanced up at me through blonde side bangs that covered most of her face.

"How can I help you, ma'am?" she asked, popping gum in her mouth.

"Hi, I am Avery Jones. I am here for...."

"Second right down the hallway. The boss is waiting for you." She pointed down the hall then went back to clacking the keys on her keyboard.

As I turned into the room, a wave of regret hit me. Why was I here? Why did I think I could do this again? I was nobody.

No one would care about or like my articles. I pushed those thoughts away. That was my old self. Those were the thoughts with him. Today I would be as great as I could be, and that was all they would expect.

"Yes, Terry, I told you the story will be phenomenal. It will show your strong and caring side. You'll skyrocket in the polls."

A woman in a sharp, tight-fitting business suit spoke briskly into the phone. Her green eyes flicked toward me as she gestured for me to sit. I obeyed at once, sliding into the chair across from her desk, trying not to look as nervous as I felt.

"I know, Terry. And you're right. I'll personally investigate that. I have to go–my newest team member just arrived. Okay. Great. Bye."

She hung up and released a long sigh, lifting her glasses onto her head before rubbing her eyes. For a moment, she looked utterly exhausted. Then, with practiced composure, she slipped her glasses back on and folded her hands in front of her.

"I swear, some of these local celebrities think they know my job better than I do," she said, her tone dripping with exasperation. The frustration melted quickly into a polished smile. "Anyway, my name's Benda, and I'm thrilled you accepted my offer. I've read some of your old articles. We could use someone with your talents."

I blinked. "Your offer? This isn't an interview?"

"No." She said as she tapped a few keys on her laptop, her green eyes flicking toward the monitor. "I'm sending your first assignment to your inbox now," she said. "We post all our stories through the digital board, but I wanted to walk you through it personally."

I straightened in my chair, trying to hide how eager I felt.

"The piece is tied to a local Civil War battle that happened just outside town," Brenda explained, sliding her glasses higher on her nose. "Our readership leans heavily male–they love history, heroism, anything with grit and sacrifice. The anniversary of Nicholas Blackstone's death is next week, so we're running a commemorative feature."

I tilted my head. "Nicholas Blackstone... the colonel?"

"That's him," she said with a short nod. "He's basically a local legend. Died young, during the final push of the battle. But before that, he did something remarkable–he was the first recorded soldier to use a form of CPR on the field. Saved a local farm boy who'd been shot and left for dead. The boy lived, went on to start a family here. People still talk about it like it's a miracle."

My pen scratched against the paper as I took notes, already picturing the story forming in my head.

"Since you live in the Blackstone Mansion," Brenda continued, "I'd start there. Readers love a personal angle. Make it feel like you're uncovering how his legacy still breathes in this town. Keep it heartfelt, not heavy. A celebration, not a history lecture."

"I can do that," I said, smiling faintly.

"Good," she replied, closing her laptop. "Your desk is next to Charles–he started last year and can fill you in on the system, photo requests, all that. And if you ever want to butter me up, large frozen coffee, hazelnut creamer."

I laughed softly as I stood. "I'll remember that."

"See that you do." She waved me toward the door. "Now go see Angie in HR to finish your paperwork and then you can get settled into your new cubicle. You can start officially on Monday. Welcome to the team, Avery."

I went up a flight of stairs toward the offices after I saw HR. She gave me all my login passwords to my computer and my credentials. She even told me that most reporters leave at 6pm, but you can stay longer when it's close to deadline time. What had likely once been several bedrooms was now open, the walls removed to form one large room. There were five desk spaces, a copy/printer machine, a small kitchenette, and a water cooler. My eyes spotted Charles next. There was an empty desk next to him. I stood up tall, marched over, and placed my bag on the desk.

"So, we meet again," I said before he could.

"I was wondering if you were going to be the new reporter." He pointed to the desk to the right of him. They were in an L shape. There was a small desk plant and a bunch of different work supplies.

I sat in my chair and swiveled for a second, taking a moment to bask in the excitement of my new chapter. I moved my laptop to the desk and arranged my other supplies. I glanced over at Charles.

"Let me guess, your first assignment is something to do with the anniversary of Nicholas Blackstone's death?"

"How did you know?" I placed my head on my knuckles.

"Everyone else turned the article down. They wanted more hard-hitting pieces."

"What is hard-hitting around here?" I asked. Charles rolled his chair over closer to me. He then looked over his shoulder, like he had a secret.

"How kids are cow-tipping more, the audacity of someone parking for fifteen minutes in a no-park zone, a strike at the local post office for a five-cent raise," he said, sitting up. I looked over at him. I wasn't sure if he was serious about those being serious crimes around here or if he was messing with me. After a few seconds, his lips started to curve upwards, then a loud laugh shot out of his mouth. He started to point at me. "You should have seen your face!"

As I looked around the office, people were staring at us. I could feel my face getting hot. I did not like people looking at me. I forced a small laugh, "Ah, yes, you got me."

"Nah, but in all seriousness, I think the biggest article we have is the one I am working on."

"What is your assignment?" I hesitantly asked. He started to tap his pen side to side on the desk.

"The animal attacks in the area. Poor out-of-towners. You best be careful; you are new here. The animals might mistake you for one." He turned back to his computer, typing away.

I spent hours researching but found little about the Blackstone residence. The hair on the back of my neck raised. I felt like eyes were watching me. I turned to see Charles leaning back in his chair.

"You look like you are on a whirlwind of research," he chuckled.

"Yeah. They have a lot of information on the web about the Civil War, but not much on the Blackstone residence." I tried pulling my eyes away from him, but it was like someone was holding my face. I could not look away.

"Well, we can talk all about it at dinner tomorrow?" Charles asked, his eyebrow rising.

My smile grew big as I blinked quickly. I was excited and scared. I didn't want to trust another man. At least not until I really knew who I was.

"I, I don't know," I said. He sat back, looking around the room. I felt like a weight had been lifted from my face, and I was able to move my head again.

"Just as colleagues," he added quickly. "I'm sorry if I came off strong. Although you are beyond beautiful, I don't date people I work with. At least not usually."

"Just as colleagues," I echoed, focusing on my laptop again.

"There's a museum near the diner that has Civil War photos," he continued. "We could check it out tomorrow."

My watch buzzed–6 p.m. The end of my first day. I turned to him with a small smile. "Okay, I'll see you tomorrow," I said, then gathered my things and headed for the stairs.

Deciding to grab dinner before heading home, I made my way to a nearby Chinese restaurant that served comfort food reminiscent of my childhood. My mom ordered Chinese once a week. As I walked, the streets were already emptying out, the town settling into the uneasy quiet that had likely become the norm since the curfew was enforced.

Outside the restaurant, a police car pulled up beside me. The window rolled down, and an officer leaned out. "Excuse me, ma'am," he called, his tone firm but not unfriendly.

I stopped and turned to face him. "Yes, Officer?"

He stepped out of the car, revealing a tall, well-built frame. His short black hair was neatly trimmed, and his dark brown eyes held a mix of authority and curiosity. It was clear he knew he was attractive, a confidence that showed in his posture.

"Just a reminder, the curfew is in effect starting at 7pm until 5am. I noticed you walking and wanted to make sure you were aware," he said, his gaze steady on mine.

"Thank you, Officer," I replied. "I'm just on my way to get some dinner before heading home. My name's Avery, by the way."

He nodded, a small smile touching his lips. "Nice to meet you, Avery. I'm Marcus."

"Nice to meet you too, Marcus," I said, returning his smile. "I appreciate the reminder."

"It's my job," he said with a slight shrug. "But I also like to ensure everyone's safety. The streets aren't the same after dark."

"I understand," I said, feeling a bit more at ease. "I won't be long, just grabbing a quick bite."

"Alright," Marcus said, his tone softening slightly. "Stay safe, and don't hesitate to call if you need anything."

"Thank you," I said again, and with a nod, he returned to his car.

As I continued my walk to the Chinese restaurant, I couldn't help but glance back at Marcus. There was something reassuring about his presence, a sense of security I hadn't felt in a while. It was a brief encounter, but it left me with a small measure of comfort as I stepped into the restaurant to order my meal.

The smell of sesame and soy sauce filled the air, grounding me as I waited for my takeout. The woman behind the counter smiled softly as she handed me the bag, the warmth of the box seeping through the paper and into my hands. For a fleeting moment, everything felt... normal.

Once outside, the night air greeted me with a sharp chill. I quickened my pace to the car, my footsteps echoing faintly on the quiet street. The town had a way of feeling both familiar and eerie after dark–too quiet, too still. I slid behind the wheel, glancing at the time glowing on the dashboard. Ten minutes until curfew.

"Come on, come on," I muttered, turning the key. The engine sputtered before catching, and relief washed over me. Streetlights blurred past as I drove, my eyes flicking between the road and the clock. Every red light felt longer than it should have, every shadow on the sidewalk a reminder that I hated driving alone at night.

When my house finally came into view, I let out the breath I hadn't realized I'd been holding. I pulled into the driveway with two minutes to spare.

The rest of the night went by smoothly. I had a love-hate relationship with the silence. I loved getting the chance to think. Something I always got in trouble doing with *him*. However, the silence also bothered me. I didn't like reliving the moments over again. I always found new ways to blame myself for everything.

I tossed and turned most of the night. I tried drinking warm milk and limiting blue light exposure. All the tricks I read about; nothing helped. I looked over at my clock. 1:00 a.m. I closed my eyes, letting my mind wander. I jumped when my cell phone chimed and grabbed it to see an unknown number calling me.

"Hello?" I asked hesitantly. Waiting for *his* voice to answer.

"Avery, I need your help," a shaky male voice said.

"Charles?" I asked.

"Yes. Please hurry," he said. The call ended. I stared at my phone for a second. It didn't make any sense. How did he get my number? Why would he call me? I wouldn't know unless I went and asked. I quickly got dressed and left.

In a blink of an eye, I was already pulling up to his house. How did I even know where he lived? I wasn't sure. This was all so strange. It was a lot bigger than my house, and darker. English Ivy overran one side of the dark brown brick home. It looked like a small castle. I didn't see any lights on through the windows.

I walked up the creaky stairs leading to the front door. The porch was a wrap-around. There was a rocking chair by the far window, and it was moving on its own. I looked behind me at a tree, but the leaves were as still as the air. I swallowed hard as I knocked hesitantly on the door. Every ounce of my body was telling me to turn around. Telling me I need to go back home.

"Avery," a faint whisper came from inside.

"Charles," I asked. I pushed on the curved black doorknob. "Hello, Charles? Where are you?"

I stuck my head inside the house. There were a lot of antiques. I could see a faint light flickering on the wall across the room. I walked inside, hesitantly. There was no noise until I approached the back of the main hallway. I could hear a crackling noise.

The light must be from a fireplace, I thought to myself. *Pull yourself together. Everything is fine.* I slowly turned the corner, and the fireplace was there in front of me. I walked into the room further to see a huge wooden desk, a black leather chair facing away from me, and someone leaning their arm against the top of the chair. Their back was facing me, as they looked out the back window, overlooking the lake.

"Charles?" I asked. The person slowly turned around. I gasped as the light from the fireplace illuminated a face I had never wanted to see again.

"Hello, Avery," Richard's gruff voice said. He picked his arm off of the back of the chair and took a few steps towards me. I stepped back, my heart starting to beat faster. The chair spun around.

"I told you she would come to me. I'm irresistible," Charles said. He licked his lips. For a brief second, it looked like he was licking his incisor. It started to protrude out of his mouth. I looked back and forth between the two as they began to laugh horrifically.

A loud chime startled me awake. I was breathing heavy and sweating, looking all around my room. I was safe inside of my bed. No one else was here. My phone continued to ring. I slowly looked over at it. The screen illuminated, showing an unknown number. *Is my dream becoming a reality?* I asked myself.

"Hello?"

Chapter 7

Avery

"Hi, is this Avery Jones?" said a male voice I didn't recognize.

"Yes, it is."

"This is Captain Lehigh from the New York Police Department. I'm sorry to call you so late, but Richard Jones posted bail last night."

My heart stopped beating. I froze in place. This was worse than the dream. This was real life.

"Avery?"

"Last night? Why the hell am I just being told?"

"I only just found out. I don't know what happened. Listen, what he did to you is unspeakable. Please save my number in your phone. If you have any questions, don't hesitate to call."

"Thanks," I said, nodding. Tears started to pour out of my eyes as I hung up. I hid under my covers, hugging one of my pillows.

Now what?

My phone read 5:00 a.m. The curfew was over, but sleep wasn't coming back anytime soon. I thought about the little diner I'd passed on my way to the interview and decided food might help clear my head. I showered and dressed quickly, but when I reached the door, something made me pause.

Do I really want to do this? If he is in this town, he will have a higher chance of finding me. What in the world am I doing? Am I really going to allow myself to keep living in fear? I survived that asshole! I am a new person. He is not going to have control over me anymore! Besides, he was always drunk. He is never going to remember my aunt's house that he had gone to one time like 10 years ago!

I took a deep breath while I grabbed the door handle. My eyes shifted back and forth until I reached my car. I glanced into the back seat before unlocking it and jumping into the front seat. My hand hit the lock button like it was a necessity, as essential as breathing. I turned the key and the clock on my dashboard flashed 6:15 a.m. I pulled out of the driveway and headed towards town.

I turned on the radio to listen to something other than my racing thoughts.

"The town is still under curfew for all residents. A fifth victim was found yesterday. Miraculously, the victim survived. When the 25-year-old woman woke up, she yelled 'bear'," a serious male's voice stated.

"Hold on, did you see the comments on the town blog?" a laughing male voice asked.

"Seriously, dude? You want to bring up the vampire part?"

"I mean, the police have never found a bear in the woods around these parts. I'm just saying, maybe the crazy explanation isn't so crazy."

I turned off the radio. I didn't want to hear about any deaths. And nothing vampire related. I mean, there was no way I could have dreamed of a vampire and then there's talk of vampires in the town! How crazy is that!

I pulled up to the local diner. It looked like a cute '70s diner you would see on TV. It was a one-floor brick building. The word DINER was huge above the door in neon pink writing. There were colorful plastic flags decorating the top of the building. Other neon signs reading "EAT" and "OPEN" hung in the windows. The food must have been good, because the place was already busy even at this early hour.

When I got inside, I couldn't help but smile. There was a young waitress escorting people to their booths. Her flawless skin seemed to glow, and something about her eyes sparkled with warmth. The busboys were even smiling and talking to other patrons. I walked up to the counter, a menu hung behind it on the wall. A sign saying "carry out" was illuminated next to it. The drinks mainly had Civil War themed names, some with the names of famous soldiers and battles.

"Hi. I'll take a black coffee and a sausage and egg breakfast sandwich," I said to the woman behind the counter. She smiled as she placed the order into the register.

"That is $8.50."

"You can keep the change," I said while handing her a $10 bill and moving to the side. I walked towards a stack of newspapers. I picked one up and walked over to the waitress.

"Would it be okay if I sat at a booth?"

"Most definitely, love." She waved her hand for me to follow her. I sat in a booth facing the front door. I could see the main road that led in and out of town. I sat there for a good ten minutes just going over the articles. I was truly impressed by how my new co-workers kept these stories so interesting. I smiled at the waitress as she brought my sandwich to the table.

I took a bite of my sandwich and then tried to turn the pages of the newspaper, but they were stuck together. I glanced up and noticed a woman watching me. Her brown eyes were wide. Her coffee mug was untouched on the table. She blinked a few times after our eyes connected. She looked down at her table and took a huge gulp of her drink. She then threw money on the table and stared at me as she left the building.

Well, that was odd, I thought to myself. *Did I spill my food on myself?* I wondered. I shrugged it off and switched between my food and flipping the pages of the newspaper. I glanced at my phone screen, as I wiped my lips. The time was now 7:30 a.m. The chime of the doorbell rang as a new customer walked in. I ducked down as I saw it was Charles. I was not ready to have a conversation with anyone. I looked behind me to see a back door. Charles was talking to the woman behind the counter, so I slid out of the booth and darted for the door. When I made it outside, I glanced back, and Charles was nowhere in sight.

"Where are you headed to this morning?" Charles asked. I gasped, turning around to face him.

He smiled, an unnerving calm in his eyes. "I didn't mean to startle you, Avery."

My heart pounded as I struggled to find words. "I was just...getting a coffee."

Charles looked back toward the diner and waved at the woman behind the counter. She smiled and waved back, then returned to her work.

"You should come back inside," Charles suggested. "I can introduce you to some of the locals."

Reluctantly, I followed him back into the diner. He walked up to the counter, engaging the waitress in conversation. "Elara, this is Avery," he said, introducing us.

Elara smiled warmly, her eyes sparkling with friendliness. "Nice to meet you, Avery."

I nodded, still trying to calm my racing heart. "Nice to meet you, too."

Charles and Elara continued chatting as I found my way back to my booth, my mind swirling with unanswered questions and a sense of foreboding. I looked up at Elara, her eyes wide as she looked at me. She looked scared talking to Charles. She seemed friendly when I was up there. I glanced at my phone, which read 7:45 a.m.

"Hey, you up to check out that museum this morning?" I asked Charles, thinking of a way to get him away from Elara. "By the time we walk to it, it'll be 8 a.m." Charles smiled and nodded, linking my arm through his as we walked out the door. I looked back at Elara, as she mouthed 'thank you.'

I enjoyed this little town. The few people I met was nice so far, a huge difference from New York. There were many historical sites here. The Confederates had marched through it several times to reach different battlefields, and Union Army support had been strong here. As the grey clouds darkened, hiding the warmth of the sun, I found myself looking everywhere, expecting Richard to show up and attack me. I didn't want anyone in my new life to know about him. Not the man he became. I wanted the old Richard. The one I fell in love with. The one who used to hold my hand while walking. The one who asked me how my day was going.

"How are you liking our little town so far?" Charles asked, breaking me free from my thoughts. He was staring at me; his pearly white teeth peeking through his lips. The color of his teeth shouldn't have bothered me this much. Why did my eyes want to keep staring at them?

"It's been a crazy experience."

"Good crazy or bad?" he asked, tilting his head to the side. His hands were behind his back as he walked. I had only ever seen people in black-and-white silent movies walk this way, never someone around my age.

"Great crazy. I have a new home and a new job. I guess I'm just a bit overwhelmed. It's been a long while since I have been on my own."

"Ah, well I am glad you are taking a liking to our town. Just know, it has some crazy quirks, but they are like any other small town."

"So, tell me more about Blackstone. Why is this town obsessed with him?" I asked, tilting my head as I looked at Charles. He chuckled.

"Well, the official story is that he fought valiantly in war but ended up dying on the battlefield. His book smarts taught the military new things back then, like first aid on the scene." Charles's shoulders stiffened as he explained.

"The unofficial story?"

"Ah, well. My great grandpa told me that while Nicholas did indeed help with first aid, and it caught the eye of his superior, he was tasked to go on a special assignment. Prior to the assignment, Nicholas left to see his wife. He wanted to tell her his great news. When he arrived, he caught her with another."

"Did he kill her or something?"

"No, he was killed on his special assignment. She lived with guilt for the rest of her life, which was about seventeen years."

"So sad, but mysterious," I stated. I looked over at Charles, who had been staring at me. Our eyes connected as he stepped into my path. A low rumble echoed in the distance.

"You're a hungry little wolf," he said, his voice calm but piercing. "You want to make a name for yourself. You don't care about the views of this town; you'll do whatever it takes to uncover the truth about Nicholas Blackstone." His eyes never blinked. The intensity in them made me want to look away, but I couldn't. Thunder cracked again, closer this time.

I let out a nervous laugh, hoping to lighten the mood. "A hungry wolf?" I repeated, tilting my head slightly.

Charles looked almost startled, as if surprised by his own words. "I just saw the glint in your eyes," he said quietly. "Thought you'd want to be the top reporter. I only hang out with the best."

I wrinkled my nose, disturbed by the ending of his sentence. "I mean, I guess it would be nice to make a name for myself," I replied with a shrug. "But I'm not looking to be a hungry wolf or dig too deep into Nicholas Blackstone. I just want a fun article to start off with." I patted his shoulder, trying to break the tension that still lingered between us.

After a few seconds, I walked around him. Ahead, a swinging metal sign read *Echoes of Battle Museum*. It wasn't far off, maybe a few buildings down. I couldn't wait to get inside, gather some basic information about this man, and then go home. It had been a weird day.

I outstretched my hand for the door handle when Charles's hand connected with it first. My eyelashes fluttered as I tried to compute how he'd arrived at the door so quickly. I hadn't heard him walking behind me. He swung the glass door open and gestured for me to enter. My lips curled up in thanks.

As we stepped inside, my mouth parted slightly as I registered how big the building was compared to how it looked from the outside. A map next to the stairs showed three levels: the basement, the floor we were on now, and an upper level.

After walking up the few steps, my eyes widened at all the artifacts from around the country. "This stuff is breathtaking. How did such a small town acquire so many things?" I asked, admiring paintings of battlefields from all over the country.

"Over the years, my family and other local families have donated what was passed down to us. Most wanted to honor those who fought here."

We wandered past cases filled with rusted rifles, dented canteens, and tattered flags. A marble statue of a soldier stood at the center of the room. He looked confident and in charge. Nearby, a bronze plaque bore the names of local men who'd fought and died in the war. The air smelled faintly of dust and polished wood, the quiet hum of the overhead lights echoing in the vaulted room.

Charles lingered near a case displaying an officer's sword and an old Union uniform. "These are authentic," he murmured, running his hand just above the glass. "Most museums only display replicas."

"Oh wow," I said softly, taking in the careful arrangement of medals, letters, and torn photographs.

A low voice interrupted the silence.

A tall and elegant man, with an air of sophistication that matched the grand setting of the museum, walked over to us.

"Hello, my name is Lucien. I am the museum's tour guide. How are you today?"

"Hello, I'm Avery Jones. It's nice to meet you. And this is Charles."

"Yes, we know each other. Hello, Lucien," Charles said, stiffening slightly. A subtle tension passed between them that I couldn't quite place.

Lucien's lips curved into a polite smile that didn't quite reach his eyes. "Charles. I didn't expect to see you... in the daylight no less."

Charles's jaw twitched. "I wear a strong SPF when it's worth my time."

Their gazes held for a moment too long before Lucien turned back to me with perfect composure, though a faint smirk lingered.

"I am doing a story on Nicholas Blackstone and the Civil War." I said, looking back and forth between the two.

"Ah, the Civil War. Follow me to the photo section," Lucien said with a smooth, almost melodic voice. "A fascinating period, full of bravery and turmoil."

He led us through another hall filled with statues and relics from the same era. A cracked drum faded regimental flags, and the solemn bust of a general with a missing ear. Lucien spoke with quiet reverence, describing how each piece had been recovered, many from old homes or battlefields long since reclaimed by nature.

"This saber belonged to a captain from the 14th Regiment," Lucien said, gesturing toward a display. "They say he refused to surrender, even after the ceasefire." His tone carried both admiration and something darker.

Then he brought us before a wall of photographs. "Now," he said, "let me show you some of the notable figures." He began pointing out various individuals in the photographs, providing detailed descriptions. As he spoke, his eyes seemed to linger a little too long on Charles, though he quickly averted his gaze whenever I noticed.

Charles, standing beside me, seemed increasingly agitated. His jaw clenched, and his eyes narrowed every time Lucien spoke. "You seem to know quite a bit about this era," Charles said, a hint of irritation in his tone. "Almost as if you lived through it yourself."

Lucien paused for a moment, a flicker of discomfort crossing his face. "One might say I've had a long time to study it," he replied carefully, glancing at Charles with a tight smile. The comment felt odd, but I dismissed it as mild mocking about his apparent love for history.

As we moved along, Lucien pointed out a series of photos featuring a group of Union Soldiers. One picture in particular caught my eye. I grabbed it and squinted, focusing on a man in the background. The resemblance was uncanny. "I swear one of the men looks just like you, Charles!" I exclaimed, pointing to the figure and looking to Charles.

Charles stepped closer, his expression hardening. He took the photo from my hand and examined it, moving it side to side. "Well, I have never had someone say that before," he muttered, his voice deepening ominously. His grip on the photo tightened, and he glanced at Lucien, who seemed to shift uncomfortably.

Lucien cleared his throat. "It's remarkable how some people resemble others from the past," he said, attempting to steer the conversation back to safer ground. "But history is full of such coincidences."

Charles ignored him, turning his intense gaze back to me. He grabbed my face gently but firmly, locking his eyes on mine. The gold specks in his irises seemed to pulse slightly, mesmerizing. My heart raced, and for a moment, I felt trapped in his stare. It reminded me of Richard and the way he used to control me, making threats and promises in the same breath.

"You will forget what you've seen. It's just a man that has some similarities to me. Perhaps an ancestor, but nothing more." Thunder crackled outside, the sudden sound breaking the spell. I blinked and took a step back, startled by the intensity of the moment. A lightning bolt illuminated the sky outside, casting eerie shadows on the walls.

"Don't touch me again. All you had to say is that you had family that lived here back then. Simple." I rubbed both sides of my cheeks. I glanced at the clock on my phone. "I think that's enough for today. We've been here for an hour already." I said, my voice shaky. I turned to Lucien, trying to maintain my composure. "Thank you, Lucien. I really enjoyed learning from you."

Lucien nodded, his expression serious. "Of course. I'm glad I could be of assistance."

Before I started to walk away, Lucien pointed once more to the man in the photograph who resembled Charles. "Some faces," he said softly, "seem to transcend time." His words sent a chill down my spine, and I couldn't shake the feeling that there was more to them than he was letting on.

Charles watched me closely, his eyes dark with unreadable emotion. "Yes, thank you, Lucien," he said, his tone flat but laced with a barely concealed annoyance. "Your...knowledge is always enlightening."

As I made my way towards the exit, Charles reached out as if to stop me but then let his hand fall to his side. His face was tense, his eyes shadowed by something I couldn't name. The air between us tightened, charged with something neither of us dared to say.

My hair brushed against my shoulders as I exited the door. I threw my hat over my head. How dare he grab me like that. My mind buzzed with confusion. The way Charles had looked at me, the way Lucien had pointedly mentioned the resemblance—it all felt strange and unsettling. I couldn't shake the feeling that there was a hidden undercurrent to everything, something just beneath the surface that I couldn't quite grasp. *Whatever Charles is hiding, I will uncover the secrets lurking in the shadows of Charles's past.*

"Avery! Wait!" Charles yelled. I guessed he wouldn't leave me alone. I spun around after the third call of my name. People looked at me as they walked past.

"I'm tired. I just want to get something to eat, go home, cook myself dinner, and relax." Lightning caressed the sky. A few raindrops hit my face and my hood. I noticed a store close by with an awning out front and slid under the cover to get out of the rain.

"I understand. I do regret grabbing you that way. I do not know what was in my head. Please, let me make it up to you. I inherited all my grandfather's items when he passed. He had Nicholas Blackstone's journals that my great grandfather passed down to him. I can find them tonight and bring them over tomorrow. See about getting you a new perspective of his life. You will have a great story. You can eat and relax while we read in silence."

His long eyelashes batted like his eyes wanted to fly away. His bottom lip slightly stuck out. I sighed. I knew I would regret this.

"Fine." I said as thunder crackled.

Charles smiled, "I'll stop by at 7 p.m."

I nodded, before we went our separate ways.

I was grateful for the rest of the day to myself. I was able to go home and force myself to get a nap in. I really needed it. It took forever for my body to relax though.

When I woke up, I realized I had nothing in the house for food or drinks and went to the store. I made sure I grabbed juice and water, but as I passed the aisle with wine and beer, I hesitated. Most hosts would have at least one bottle for their guests, but I didn't want any of that near me. After years of abuse from Richard, I'm taking my life back over.

The next day, my mood was a lot better. I still tossed and turned all night and was still worried about Richard finding me and freaked out by Charles's aggressiveness but today was a new day.

I made chicken noodle soup and a pot pie. For dessert I made an apple pie. I finished up just as I heard a loud bang outside. I jumped, wondering if it could be Richard. I moved the curtain slightly to see a truck pulling into the driveway and parking next to my car. Charles exited the driver's seat. He was wearing a tight black t-shirt that showed his muscles underneath. I licked my lips as the thought of taking his shirt off amused me slightly. I shook my head and walked out onto the patio.

"Wow, I haven't been to this house in so long." He said.

"Why were you here? Did you know my aunt?"

"Just by reputation. She was a lovely lady. I had been here a few times for the reenactments they used to throw in her backyard."

"She loved those things. Any time she could throw a party, she wanted to be the head of it." I smiled, looking around. Charles walked up the patio steps and stood in front of me, giving me a half smile. I turned to grab the front door handle. "Would you like something to drink? I don't have alcohol, but I bought juice and water."

"I'd love water," he murmured, stepping close enough that his breath grazed my ear. The hairs on my neck rose in warning.

Chapter 8

Nicholas

I jolted awake, my heart pounding in my chest. I looked around, recognizing my home. I was in the living room. It was eerily quiet, the house empty. I rubbed my eyes, trying to shake off the remnants of sleep. The silence was suffocating, an oppressive blanket over the familiar surroundings.

I got up and began to wander through the house, room by room, but no one was there. The absence of life, of Emily, gnawed at me, an emptiness that felt more pronounced with each step. Every corner, every piece of furniture held a memory, a ghost of the past that haunted me relentlessly.

Desperation clawed at me. I needed to find Emily. I couldn't stay here, in this echo of a life that once was. With a determined breath, I headed for the front door. As I stepped outside, the air felt heavy, almost tangible. I walked down the steps and out onto the path, the house shrinking behind me.

But no sooner had I taken a few steps than I found myself back inside the cave. Confusion hit me like a wave. Determined, I pushed forward, leaving the cave and forcing my way through the tangled woods, branches snapping against my arms as I ran. I broke through the tree like and sprinted toward the edge of the property, every muscle in my body screaming to escape. I tried again, my heart pounding harder with each stride–yet the moment I thought I was free, the world shifted. In an instant, the forest dissolved, and I was standing once more within the same cold, suffocating walls of the cave.

Frustration boiled over. I tried multiple times, each attempt more frantic than the last. No matter which direction I chose, no matter how fast or slow I moved, I always ended up back in the cave. It was as if an invisible force was keeping me prisoner.

"How will I ever find Emily now?" I shouted into the emptiness, my voice echoing back at me. The hopelessness of my situation began to sink in, a heavy weight settling in my chest. I collapsed onto the ground, my head in my hands.

The cave's darkness felt suffocating, an inescapable void. I thought of Emily, her smile, her touch, the life we had shared. The future we would have with our child. How could I ever reach her if I couldn't even leave this place? Anger and despair mingled within me, a volatile mix that threatened to consume me.

"Emily!" I screamed her name, my voice breaking. "Emily, where are you?"

Again, the only response was the hollow echo of my own voice, bouncing off the cave walls. I felt a tear roll down my cheek, followed by another. I was trapped, lost, and more alone than I had ever been. I wasn't a soldier on the battlefield anymore–I wasn't even a man of flesh and blood. I was a ghost, a relic of the past, and somehow stranded in a future that wasn't mine. The weight of that truth pressed on me as heavily as the cave walls.

In the midst of my despair, a faint memory surfaced. Emily's voice, soft and soothing, telling me to never give up. To always keep fighting. I clung to that memory, letting it anchor me. I wouldn't give up. I couldn't. For Emily and our baby, I would find a way out of this nightmare.

Taking a deep breath, I stood up. I needed a plan, a new approach. There had to be a way to break free, to find Emily. I wiped the tears from my face, a newfound determination settling in. I would keep trying, keep searching. For Emily, I would do anything.

A noise echoed through the cave, a sharp contrast to the silence within. I turned, straining to listen, my heart pounding in my chest. As I moved closer to the cave's entrance, I could make out the sound of footsteps crunching on the gravel outside.

Slowly, I emerged from the shadows and stepped into the dim light filtering in. I saw a man standing there, his back turned to me, engaged in a conversation with Avery. I inched closer, until I was behind him. He turned towards me, showing his full features.

"Charles?" I whispered, disbelief flooding my senses. How was he here? The familiarity of his features sent a wave of shock and fear through me. *Maybe he knows where Emily is.*

My excitement surged, but then a memory struck me like a lightning bolt. The letter I had found in the cave. The words seemed to burn in my mind: "...stop Charles at all costs."

I took a step back, my joy tainted by the grim reminder. What did it mean? My heart pounded as the realization settled in. I had to be careful. Very careful.

I crept closer through the shadows and watched as Avery and Charles walked towards the house. Avery struggled with her keys, then stepped into the house. I followed her quickly, then turned back to see Charles lingering at the threshold, his expression unreadable. I squinted, trying to decipher the reason for his hesitation. Then, in an instant, his eyes turned black, veins spidering out from their corners in a web of darkness. A cold shiver ran down my spine as I saw the transformation, a grotesque mask that vanished as quickly as it appeared when Avery turned around.

He spoke, his voice calm yet demanding. "Avery, you need to invite me in properly."

Avery frowned, confused. "What do you mean, Charles? You're already here."

Charles smiled, but it didn't reach his eyes. "No, I mean, you have to say the words. Invite me in."

The atmosphere grew tense, the air thick with unspoken truths. Avery hesitated, clearly unsettled. "Alright, Charles. Please, come in," she said, her voice wavering slightly.

I couldn't tear my gaze away from Charles as he finally stepped inside, his demeanor returning to normal. But the image of his blackened eyes and the sinister veins haunted me. It triggered a memory of the night I had seen Charles's teeth lengthen into fangs, right before everything went dark. Right before I died.

The truth slammed into me with the weight of cannon fire. Charles wasn't just cruel or powerful–he was something inhuman. A vampire. The word echoed in my head, impossible yet undeniable, explaining the shadows in his gaze, the unnatural strength, the reason he still walked this earth long after my bones should have outlasted his. I had faced death on battlefields, but this revelation chilled me deeper than any musket or bayonet ever could.

My death replayed in my mind with vivid clarity. The pain, the betrayal, the cold embrace of death. It all rushed back, a torrent of fear and anger that I struggled to contain.

Another memory surged forward, unbidden. The little boy, and my hands pressing rhythmically on his small chest, desperation clawing at my heart. He had been so still, so lifeless. Charles had been there too, holding the boy's head with an intensity that seemed out of place.

I remembered the look in Charles's eyes, the way they had glinted with something dark and unspoken. And then, miraculously, the boy had gasped, his eyes fluttering open. At the time, I had thought it was a stroke of luck, a miracle even. But now, with the memory of Charles's transformation at the door fresh in my mind, I couldn't shake the suspicion that there was more to it.

Had Charles used his vampire venom to bring the boy back to life? Was that even possible? The questions swirled in my mind, each one more troubling than the last. The boy had lived, but at what cost? And what did that mean for Charles? For all of us?

"Make yourself at home," she said, gesturing toward the living room. "I'll grab those drinks."

Charles nodded and walked to the dining table, where he spread out my journals. The sight of them brought a pang of nostalgia and a surge of curiosity. What secrets had I recorded in those pages? What memories had I preserved?

Avery returned with two glasses of juice, setting them down as Charles began to leaf through one of my journals. I hovered nearby, invisible but very much present, listening to their conversation with bated breath.

"Find anything interesting?" Avery asked, settling into a chair across from him.

Charles looked up, a faint smile on his lips. "There's a lot here. Nicholas was quite the chronicler."

My memories, my thoughts, all laid bare for them to see.

Charles's voice was steady as he spoke of the war. "My great grandfather told me Nicholas was a brave soldier, but he was also a loving husband. His wife, Emily, the light of his life. She died tragically years after he passed."

The mention of Emily sent a wave of sorrow through me. My beloved Emily—our time together stolen far too soon. We had always dreamed of growing old side by side, of leaving this world hand in hand after long, full lives. But instead, our life had ended in ways we never could have imagined.

"Emily died years after Nicholas," Charles continued. "She took her own life."

I recoiled, my ghostly form flickering with anguish. Suicide? My Emily? I had never suspected. The revelation was a dagger to my already wounded heart.

"Why did she feel guilty?" Avery asked, her voice barely a whisper.

Charles hesitated, his gaze meeting hers. "Emily missed Nicholas terribly, but she also felt immense guilt. She had betrayed him."

The room seemed to freeze. I moved closer, my anger and disbelief palpable even in my spectral state. A memory surged forward, unbidden: Charles and Emily kissing before I was killed. My mind reeled. Could it be true?

"You killed her, didn't you?" I demanded silently, knowing they couldn't hear me. My mind was awhirl with suspicions and half formed conclusions.

"I remember," I whispered to myself, the scene replaying vividly in my mind. Charles and Emily, lips together, but something about her eyes, the vacant glaze, told me she wasn't truly herself. The ache of betrayal tore through me, though I couldn't tell if it was meant for Charles who took advantage, or Emily not pushing him away. The memory blurred into the cold realization of what came next–my death.

I watched Charles, my anger growing as he continued his charade. "She carried that guilt with her for years until it became unbearable."

I knew that he was lying. I felt it in the very core of my being. I could feel the rage boiling within me, my ghostly presence flickering with intensity. I knew Emily used to write in journals like me. I needed to find those journals. With a heavy heart, I retreated into the shadows, a silent witness to the lies that had been spoken.

Avery

Charles and I read journal after journal for hours. My lips stretched out in a yawn, and I looked at my phone. The screen read midnight.

"You must be exhausted. I will leave the journals here with you." Charles said, walking towards the door.

"Are you sure?" I asked.

He nodded. "Positive. It's not like I don't know where you live." Charles and I chuckled. He grabbed my hand and gently kissed it before leaving. I watched as his truck left the driveway. I closed the door and went back to the dining table; the journals of Nicholas Blackstone still spread out before me. The weight of the revelations Charles shared from his great-grandfather pressed heavily on my heart. Emily's tragic end, shrouded in guilt and sorrow, haunted my thoughts. I felt a deep, aching sadness for her—a woman torn apart by grief and the unbearable burden of her betrayal. Emily had loved Nicholas deeply, and the idea that she had carried such pain with her until the end was almost too much to bear.

Charles's departure left an unsettling silence in the house. His stories had been a reminder of the past and the dark secrets entwined with this place. His story about Emily seemed like a whispered rumor passed down through generations. It was hard to separate fact from fiction, and the ambiguity gnawed at the edges of my mind.

I couldn't shake the feeling that there was more to uncover, more truths hidden in the folds of the past. Emily's death and the vague rumors Charles recounted all pointed to a deeper, darker narrative. I felt a responsibility to uncover it–not just as a reporter chasing a story, but as someone who knew what it was like to have her truth buried under someone else's lies. I couldn't stand the thought of Emily being silenced forever. As I closed the journals and prepared to put them away, I promised myself that I would find out the truth–for Emily, for Nicholas, and maybe even the part of me still searching for justice.

The words on the page blurred together. My eyes grew heavier with every line, my head bobbing before I caught myself. I blinked hard, trying to refocus. Somewhere in the quiet house, a faint thumb echoed. My head jerked up, my heart lurching into my throat. For a panicked second, I thought someone had broken in. But then I realized the sound had only been the journal sliding off my lap, and the sudden chill in the room told me I had dozed off without meaning to.

Rubbing my face, I reached to gather the fallen book, determined to finish at least the last few pages. That was when something shifted in the corner of my vision. A glimmer of light hit my peripheral. Slowly, I turned my head toward the living room. The fireplace roared to life, flames dancing wildly in the hearth. With each flicker of orange and gold, my body tensed. Fire was one thing I didn't like to have around me. How did this turn on?

"Hello, Avery." A slurred, deep voice came from behind me. Lightning struck loudly as I turned around, my shoulders tensing with every breath. The next flash of lightning illuminated the shadow I feared seeing again.

"Richard."

It felt like an eternity before I could find any words. Empty cans of beer littered the floor. How the fuck did he find me? *How long has he been* here? I asked myself. Richard belched and crushed a can between his fingers, the noise echoing in the room. My clean floor was now covered with empty cans.

"I know your mother taught you better, she would have a panic attack if she saw all these cans on the floor." I said, trying not to show how scared I was of him.

"It's a good thing she ain't here, isn't it?" His laughter grew in the stale air around me. "You need to get some more for me. Use the money you stole to leave."

"First off, that was *my* money from all the hard work I did. Secondly, I'm not leaving *my* home in the middle of a storm to get you more beer when you're the one who needs to leave." I pointed furiously at the door. My chest rose and fell faster with each second he stared at me. I wished I knew what he was thinking.

"New home, new confidence, eh?" he said, standing up and chuckling. He stumbled over to the table near me. There was a sandwich on top of it. My mind screamed to run out the door before he could get to me, but my heart urged me to stay and fight for my freedom. I didn't know which to follow. My body was frozen in time. He turned his head back, a sly smile crossing his face, and hurled his sandwich at my face.

"Who the fuck do you think you are? You're still that scared little mouse, and this tiger isn't done playing with you yet." He lept towards me, gripping my arms. "If I can't have you, no one else will. And after tonight, you will be thrown in one of those empty graves, next to me forever." He looked out the window, and as lightning cracked against the ground outside, it illuminated two empty graves in the yard. "I will not go back to jail, and you will always be with me."

My fight-or-flight instinct kicked in. I couldn't escape his grip, so I jammed my knee into his crotch. A yelp of pain filled the air. I ran towards the front door, but he grabbed my foot, knocking me halfway out of the house. I kicked back, his hand losing control. My mind went blank as I clamored to my feet. Before I could take a step, a sharp pain struck my left cheek, and I lost balance, falling down the stairs. Through the blur of tears and shock, I caught sight of Richard moving toward the door, following me outside as if nothing had happened. The thunder rumbled louder. I rolled onto my back, and he stood over me.

"Forever mine," Richard laughed, raising his hand. This was going to be it. I couldn't fight anymore. I would only be free of him when he killed me. I closed my eyes.

A scream tore through the night–his scream. A cacking boom followed, shaking my ears. I snapped my eyes open just in time to see a flash of light slam into Richard. His body jerked unnaturally, back arched like a puppet on invisible strings, before he crumpled to the ground beside me.

I couldn't move. My chest heaved, my pulse pounding in my throat. His eyes stared blank and glassy, his chest still.

Oh God. Is he dead? Did that really just happen? I crawled closer on trembling hands, my breath shallow. "Richard?" The name scraped out of me like broken glass. No response. I pressed my palm to his chest, waiting for even the faintest rise and fall. Nothing.

My stomach churned. A sob burst from me. Relief. Horror. Confusion. Was I free, or about to pay for this with my life? The night seemed to mock me with its silence until thunder cracked so close it rattled my bones. A tree split open outside, lightning sparking fire through the rain.

The world jolted back into motion. Shaking, I forced myself to my feet, stumbling toward the house. My hands fumbled with my purse until I yanked out my phone and dialed 911.

"911, what is your emergency?" the operator's voice buzzed in my ear.

I turned to the window, lightning spilling across the yard. My breath caught in my throat. Richard's body was gone.

$$Chapter\ 9$$

Nicholas

My eyes rocketed open as a blow of air filled my lungs. Rain was hitting my face. Lightning streaked across the sky, and my whole-body shook. For a moment, I lay still, blinking against the downpour, convinced I had only just awoken from some horrible dream. The cave couldn't have been real. It had to be the product of an overworked mind, a nightmare that clung to me like smoke.

I tried to raise myself up as quickly as I could, but it felt like a boulder was holding me down. My chest heaved with the effort, and doubt crept in. Why did my limbs feel so heavy? I shook my head. No. It was just a dream. I took a few deep breaths, then forced myself up to a sitting position.

"What the hell?" a male voice said.

I quickly looked around me. I was not alone. "Hello, who is there?"

I gasped as the same male voice came out of my mouth. My heart stopped. That wasn't possible. I clutched my throat. What was going on? Was I sick? I had never heard my voice like this before. Oh no, I hoped I didn't have typhoid fever. I looked all over my body for any marks. My arms were oddly harrier and larger than I remembered. The clothes I wore were not my own either. I would never be seen in public wearing an undershirt and whatever these denim pants were.

A desperate thought clawed through me. Emily. I needed to find her. She would know what was happening.

I staggered to my feet, the ground lurching like the deck of a ship. Each step felt unsteady, unnatural, as if my body didn't quite belong to me. A burning sensation erupted in my stomach, and I lurched forward, gripping the side of the house as my insides emptied into the bushes.

When I finally raised my head, the night pressed in, silent except for the patter of rain. I mustered all my energy to go to the front door once more.

"Emily. My love. Are you home?" I yelled.

"Get away from my house, you psycho!" a woman's voice yelled through the door. That did not sound like my love. Who was in there with her? My feet stumbled on the steps. My palms felt the cold stone as I tried not to faceplant.

"Emily! Come to the door at once! It is I, Nicholas! Your husband!" My body stood still. Why was I shouting at her like that? I never raised my voice to her. She would never allow me to. She would have fought back with me.

I finally pulled myself up to the front door. My hand grasped the cold metal of the doorknob. My eyes raised up to the glass when the door would not budge. My legs instinctively took a few steps back, ready to fight. What man was in my home with my wife?

I raised my arm to point my finger when the person inside did the same movement. Now he was mocking me! How rude indeed! The wind blew my hair into my face. I looked at the man in front of me. His medium brown hair was also caressing his face. But how could this be? He was inside the house.

"Emily!" I yelled, and the person's mouth moved. His nose wrinkled when he stretched his mouth open, mirroring my actions. I didn't understand this. There was no way this man could be mimicking me. The boards under my feet cracked. My hands raised, touching the glass. It was not another man at all, but my reflection. But how?

And then, a memory jolted through me. The lightning's blinding strike tearing the sky open as my body fell into someone else. Into the man hurting the woman inside my house. His body swallowed mine, as if the storm itself had forced my soul into his flesh.

My stomach twisted as the truth rooted itself. I was trapped inside of Richard's body!

Red and blue light splashed across the yard, blinding me. A strange carriage rolled to a stop, its wheels hissing and crunching against the gravel, though I saw no horses pulling it. A tall man stepped out, his hand already resting on the small black weapon at his hip. His hat shadowed his brow, but the metallic gleam on his chest caught my eye. A star.

"Sir, step away from the house!" His voice commanded. "Hands where I can see them."

I froze, my palms lifting slowly into the air, obeying the man behind the badge I knew too well. Sheriffs wore them as a mark of authority.

"Identify yourself," he barked, taking a few steps closer.

"Nicholas Blackstone, sir." I yelled back.

"I'm Sheriff Radley. We got a call about a disturbance. I'm going to search your body now. Keep your hands up where I can see them," he ordered, stepping closer to me. I nodded and he slid his hands along my body.

After he patted me down, he took a few steps back. I tilted my head as my eyes slid to the weapon at his side. "Where did you get a riffle that small?"

The sheriff's jaw tightened. "It's a handgun. And I'd rather not use it. Don't make me."

I blinked at the odd contraption. "Did the government issue it straight from the armory? Perhaps General Grant himself put it in your hand?"

Sheriff Radley's eyes narrowed as if I'd spoke nonsense. "No, sir. Have you been drinking tonight?"

"Ale?" I frowned. "I have not had a drop! Unless..." My head swam, the world wobbling under my feet. "At least I do not remember drinking any."

"Easy there, sir." Why don't you take a seat on the steps?" Sheriff Radley's voice was calm but firm, his hand never straying from his weapon. He gestured toward the stairs with a sharp motion. "Sit down. Now."

I obeyed, though my legs wobbled like sea-worn ropes. My bottom landed heavily on the steps. The door behind me creaked open, and a young woman stepped out. Her reddish-brown curls tumbled around her face, her blue eyes glistening with tears. My heart lurched at the sight of her distress, though I could not understand why I felt such blame tightening in my chest.

Pain throbbed behind my eyes. I pressed my hands over them, and in the darkness, images burst forth–her face streaked with blood, fear widening her eyes as she fled. *Please, Richard. I love you. Why do you have to be this way?*

The voice echoed in my mind. Rage exploded through me. I shot to my feet, a scream ripping free of my throat.

"Whoa! Stay calm." The sheriff's voice was iron now, one hand raised, the other resting on the grip of his sidearm. He angles his head, speaking into the radio clipped to his shoulder. "Dispatch, this is 3574. I've got a volatile subject. Bringing him in."

"I just want my Emily," I pleaded, desperation cracking my voice. "Please, let me see her. This is our home."

The woman's face twisted, her tears spilling over. "Emily? Like Emily Blackstone?" She asked. I nodded my head. "Richard, stop messing with me. You are not a Blackstone. This is *my* house."

Her words stunned me, Richard? Why was she calling me that?

"I beg your pardon, madam," I stammered. "You must be mistaken. I have lived here all my life. I serve the Union Army, and this is my wife's house. And this is your gratitude?"

Her eyes widened with fear. She glanced at the sheriff, who tilted his head slightly, one eyebrow arched.

"You're telling me you're a Civil War soldier?" His tone was clipped, skeptical.

I straightened, clinging to what pride I had left. "A scholar first, but yes, I've been serving these last few months."

The sheriff's lips curled into a mirthless laugh. "Well, good news. The Union won. About 150 years ago."

My jaw clenched. "Now you mock me as well. What kind of peacekeeper are you?"

"The kind who's trying to keep this calm," Sheriff Radley snapped. "But you're digging yourself deeper by the second."

My fists tightened, nails biting into my palms. Red and blue lights swelled brighter as more deputies showed up. My pulse quickened as I watched all their eyes on me, placing their hands on similar black weapons like Sheriff Radley.

"We'll take you to the station. You'll get a cot, maybe some rest, and we'll figure out who you are."

The woman sobbed again, the flashing lights painting her face red and blue. For a moment, through the blur of my spinning head, I felt I knew her. Pain spiked behind my eyes, and I pressed my palms to them.

"Sir, are you okay?" Radley's voice blended into hers. Softer now, almost tender. A hand touched my shoulder. Electricity coursed through me at the contact. I lowered my hands—and in the glow of the lights, her face blurred, shifted, and for a heartbeat... it was Emily. Her blue eyes sparkled at me and the way she smiled while pushing her hair behind her ear, made me tingle. Her auburn hair was pinned up on the top of her head. Suddenly, the other woman's face appeared again.

"Emily! Emily, come back!" I yelled out. Other officers yanked my hands behind my back and clipped something metal around my wrists.

"Calm down, sir. Do not resist," Sheriff Radley said in a calm voice. The officers handed me to him, and he ushered me over to the metal contraption they arrived in. He opened the back door, and his cold hand pushed me inside it.

"Sir, this is so outrageous that you would think I, Nicholas Blackstone, would be crazy!"

"So, you're telling me that you're a 150-year-old war hero?" he asked, tilting his head, trying not to smile. I honestly had nothing to respond to that. If I didn't know myself, I would think I sounded crazy too. But if it had really been 150 years, how did I come back?

"I guess it would sound crazy from your perspective, but I am telling you I am no liar or loon. I am who I say I am."

"Call me the Easter Bunny then."

I opened my mouth to respond, but the sheriff slammed the door. My reflection in the window showed a disheveled man in his mid-twenties. His medium brown hair was sticking up everywhere. I needed to figure out how to get out of this body. I could not understand how anyone could allow themselves to look this way. The sheriff got in the front of the metal contraption after he spoke to the woman. He glanced back at me, then turned around and grabbed a circular object. My body shifted slightly side to side when the contraption started to move.

"What is going on here? Wait, is this an automobile?" My mind started to race with a thousand questions. The sheriff sighed heavily.

"That's correct. And how would you know that if you were from the Civil War era? Automobiles weren't invented yet."

"I had read some reports about a German engineer planning to make one prior to the war. His ideas were extraordinary."

"Well, he made it. Look, you would save yourself a lot of trouble and agony if you would just stop the act and start talking to me."

"What would you like to talk to me about? How I went to see my wife prior to getting a special assignment from my commander just to see her making out with my comrade Charles? Or how I died fighting him? I have absolutely no idea what is going on with Emily and our marriage. And now you are telling me I am in an automobile, and I need to stop lying to you?"

"If you want to keep playing the lies, fine. Let's play. If you did die back in, what year was it?"

"1862."

"What side did you say you were on?"

"I was a soldier for the Union."

"Ah, good, you were on the winning side!" His voice rose slightly, pretending like I was winning something. My annoyance level rose with every second I spent with this man. I did not understand why I could not go see my wife.

"Wait, if I died and you say it's been 150 years, what happened to my wife?"

"Well, honestly, I never heard you had a wife, even during the countless big parties the community has had in your name. Ugh, now you have me saying 'you.' You know what, I am tired of helping you. Why don't you just use your right to stay silent for the rest of the car ride." The sheriff's attitude changed from inquisitive to annoyed faster than this automobile was going. I wondered what happened to my wife. Why has no one ever heard of her? This was indeed a mystery. I hope she was not hurt by Charles.

We finished the ride in silence. We pulled up to a building with more sheriff automobiles. They all looked the same besides the numbers on them. Things had certainly changed since my day. The sheriff opened my door and walked me into this high brick building. My neck craned so high that it twinged in sharp pain. I had not realized I stopped to look until the sheriff pushed me.

"C'mon." he said. "I have tons of paperwork to do."

"What kind of paperwork?"

"Paperwork on how ridiculous you are," he said. I wanted to yell at him, but at this point, I was exhausted. This body was still getting sober. I just wanted a nice cot to lay on. He walked me into a cell. A wave of happiness rushed over me when I saw the cot.

"Thank heavens," I said out loud. The sheriff looked at me but did not say a word. He motioned his fingers in a circular motion, to have me turn away from him. I did. I could hear some slight rattle as the cuffs around my wrist loosened. I pulled my arms in front of me, rubbing the light pink marks left on my wrists. A loud clanking noise startled me. The sheriff was on the other side of the metal bars.

"Try to get some rest. Maybe when you've had time to sober up, you'll think more clearly about who you are."

Chapter 10

Avery

The silky sheets on my bed couldn't mask the hellish night I had endured. I had twisted and turned for hours after the police left. Shouldn't I feel relieved that he's back in jail? The question gnawed at me, but no answer came.

I turned my head to see the red digital alarm clock on my nightstand read 5:45 a.m. "Shoot," I muttered to myself. "Might as well go for a run." Maybe the fresh air would clear my head.

I quickly changed into my running gear and headed for the door. As I stepped outside, the cool morning air hit my face, and I took a deep breath. Just as I started to stretch, a pair of glowing eyes caught my attention from the edge of the woods. My heart skipped a beat.

Before I could react, a figure emerged from the shadows. It was Marcus, one of the sheriff deputies. I let out a startled gasp.

"Sorry to scare you," Marcus said, stepping closer. "I was just checking the woods after we arrested your ex. Wanted to make sure he didn't leave anything behind. We never seen a car. You shouldn't be running out here alone."

"I was just having a hard time sleeping," I admitted, still trying to steady my racing heart. Marcus covered his mouth, yawning. "Would you like a coffee?"

Marcus nodded. "Sure, that sounds good."

I led him inside and started brewing a pot of coffee. As the rich aroma filled the kitchen, I couldn't help but ask, "Have there been any updates on the killings?"

Marcus shook his head. "Same information you hear on the radio. The official cause is believed to be animal attacks."

"If I go by what I have heard on the radio, they are saying vampires," I said, laughing. Marcus paused, his expression unreadable.

"I can't go into any more details."

I handed him a cup of coffee. "How long have you been a police officer?"

"A few years now," he replied, taking a sip. "I like the idea of helping people, keeping the community safe. Plus, the camaraderie with the other officers. Nothing like having a pack of friends by your side every day."

We chatted for a bit longer, sharing small talk. Just as I was starting to feel more at ease, Marcus's radio crackled to life. He listened intently for a moment, then stood up.

"Sorry, duty calls," he said, heading for the door.

"Stay safe," I called after him as he left.

As the door closed behind him, I couldn't shake the feeling that there was more to the story than Marcus was letting on.

I showered and ate a quick, small breakfast. My appetite had vanished amid the chaos. Within the hour, I was singing along to music in my car, hoping it would lift my spirits.

"That was the latest hit from Taylor Swift. Now, for some local news," the radio deejay announced. "Deputies found the mauled body of another tourist. The sheriff's department is asking residents to stay inside after dark and follow the curfew. They believe it to be some kind of rabid animal."

The radio continued to play in the background as my mind wandered. Deaths always unsettled me, regardless of the cause.

I pulled into a parking spot. I flipped down my sun visor, inspecting my teeth and skin in the mirror. My long brownish-red hair was behaving, styled in a half-up do that I had carefully curled to frame my face. I closed my eyes for a moment, taking a slow, deep breath. My thoughts drifted to Richard, rotting in his jail cell. I exhaled slowly, opened my eyes, and forced a smile.

"You got this, Avery. You're better without him. Let's show him and the whole world who the hell you are!" A genuine smile crept across my face.

The clanking of my heels halted as I tripped up the steps. I hadn't worn these black heels in years—Richard didn't like me being taller than him. Wearing them now felt like a declaration. Screw you, Richard. This is my life! I can be as short or tall as I choose now!

My desk was beside Charles's. I was grateful for his help yesterday, but after that dream of him and Richard working together and then Richard actually showing up, I was thankful he wasn't at his desk yet. Maybe he would stay out in the field. I placed my purse inside my desk and swiveled around in my chair.

"Oh my God, Charles! You scared me!" My skin crawled as his face hovered over his knuckles on my desk. "When did you get there?"

"Why don't we work together on your story?" Charles asked. Our eyes met, and I felt an inexplicable urge to stare into them. I blinked rapidly, convinced his pupils were changing sizes. I turned to my laptop, powering it on. When I glanced back at Charles, his eyes were narrowed.

"How are you not...?"

"Not what?" I asked, glancing up at him. His mouth opened slightly, revealing his super white teeth. His body language shifted, and he cocked his head to the side, displaying a charming smile.

"Most reporters here would be begging to work with me because of all my awards in the last year. Yet, you don't. What did I do to offend you?" he asked, his tone condescending. My cheeks warmed, and the coldness in his eyes triggered a memory of Richard.

Richard had gone to his parents' house to do yard work. They lived in a huge, expensive house and rarely hired help. His father had serious trust issues, always fearing theft or worse. I stayed home to do my daily chores, scrubbing the tiles on my hands and knees for hours. Richard didn't want any carpet in the house. When he returned, covered in mud from head to toe, he slammed the front door shut and threw his tool belt down, walking through the house to the upstairs.

"Richard!" I yelled from the kitchen, having just finished the last of the dishes. I walked into the living room, where muddy boot prints indicated someone had been there. My face boiled with anger. My mind went blank as my body hit the floor. A throbbing ache spread across the back of my head. My neck cranked up just as another blow landed on my face. Richard's hardened eyes locked onto mine.

"I thought you were going to have this house spotless by the time I got back," he yelled, stepping closer. My body shivered.

"I had it cleaned. That's from your boots," I murmured. His hand collided with my cheek, turning my face. My chest ached from the rapid breathing. I didn't know what happened next. It felt like I left my own body. I remember seeing myself rising from the ground and lunging at him. My body collided with the wall when he sidestepped. His laugh echoed in my mind.

"Now, clean that up." He pointed to the mud. I went to grab the mop, but he yanked my arm behind me, grabbing my face. "Clean. That. Up. With. Your. Mouth."

"W-what?" I stuttered. Before I could comprehend his words, my head was forced to the ground. Emotions overwhelmed me. Tears streamed down my face as mud covered it. I tried grabbing his arm, but he was unmovable. I held my breath, trying not to inhale the dirt.

"Next time, you won't talk back to me!" He pushed harder before letting go. I sobbed, wiping mud from my face. "Stupid bitch."

Charles placed his hand on my shoulder, snapping me back to the present.

"Are you okay?" Charles asked, his eyes fixed on me.

"I am. Honestly, I'm just overwhelmed. I appreciate your help, but I need to do this story on my own. It's my first story. We can collaborate on a future one." I turned back to my laptop and started to do some research.

I could hear Charles slide back into his chair and typing on his computer. I took a quiet breath, my shoulders relaxing. I hoped I hadn't hurt his feelings, but I had to be truthful.

I researched the Civil War period. What people were like. What did they do in their day-to-day lives. Favorite clothes for the time. My eyes started to blur and I looked at my phone screen. It said 11 a.m. I was starving and thirsty and needed a break for my eyes. I turned to look at Charles who was typing away on his computer with headphones on. I was going to ask if he wanted anything, but starting conversation may make him want to come out with me. I grabbed my purse from the drawer and headed towards the elevator.

As I entered the elevator with four other people, I turned around and noticed Charles was gone from his computer. My eyes scanned the office, but he was nowhere in sight. How does he move around so quickly?

I was the last to exit the elevator. I started walking down the street; the museum wasn't far from our office. I could stop there before I grabbed lunch. The hair on the back of my neck stood up. A feeling of dread washed over me. I glanced behind to see Charles standing outside the building, just watching me. I quickened my pace and glanced again, but he wasn't there.

A block down, my stomach churned. I looked back and saw him separated from me by two people. I quickly ducked into the nearest shop without even noticing its appearance. I leaned against the brick wall next to the door, my heart racing. I stood there for a moment, looking up to see a mirror across from me. I watched for Charles to pass by, but he never did. Was I imagining things? I let out a sigh of relief. Turning towards the door, I saw Charles standing on the opposite side. I pressed back against the brick wall, crouching down as tears welled up in my eyes.

"I see you, Avery. Why are you hiding from me?" he demanded. I looked up at the mirror, but couldn't see him there.

"What the...?" I whispered. I peeked around the corner. Charles slammed his fist into the door.

"You cannot hide in there forever. You will eventually need to talk to me.," he shouted through the door, hitting it once more before walking away. My body shook as I leaned against the wall, letting out the breath I had been holding.

Finally, I composed myself and stood up, taking in my surroundings for the first time. A blend of aromas hit my nose all at once—sage, vanilla, lavender, and some scents I couldn't identify. Shelves lined one wall, filled with bottles of herbs and wax candles beside them. Across from me, a wall displayed an array of relics: eyeballs preserved in jars, rabbit feet, golden crosses, a replica of a pharaoh's head in statue form, and more. My head spun with a mix of intrigue and unease.

I bent down to examine some items on the lower shelves. A fairy skeleton encased in a glass jar caught my eye. *Probably something you'd find on a movie set,* I thought, a skeptical smile tugging at my lips. Magic in films had always fascinated me–incantations, flying books, fire from fingertips–but I'd never believed any of it was real. A small part of me wished it could be, though. Real magic would mean there was more to the world than pain and loss. But wishing and believing were two very different things.

I navigated around the shelves, glancing at odd bottles filled with unique items. Some looked cheap and theatrical, while others... others felt unsettling authentic. My stomach churned at the sight of a jar containing a heart. *Movie props don't usually smell this strong,* I reminded myself, though my doubt wavered.

Trying to distract myself, I brushed my fingers against an old tapestry hanging on the wall. A glint of gold behind it caught my attention. Curiosity piqued, I moved the tapestry aside to reveal a beautifully crafted triangular door set into the wall. The gold hue shimmered strangely, unlike any metal I'd ever seen, and the inside of the triangle was a deep, impossible red.

My fingers grazed the door and something stirred in me. It wasn't nerves this time. It was power. A heat that rolled up from the pit of my stomach and out through my fingertips and the door split open in the middle, swinging backwards to reveal a dark room. As I stepped inside, lights flickered on automatically. My mouth opened slightly when I saw a book floating in the air. I shook my head. *This can't be real. Did I hit my head?*

My eyes widened in amazement as I took in the rest of the hidden library. This must be the store's private collection.

Dim light cast long shadows on the ancient tomes, and the air was thick with the scent of aged paper. I walked along the shelves, running my fingers over the spines of countless volumes, feeling a strange sense of connection. A section of red books caught my eye. One book stood out, a brighter shade of red than the others. Carefully, I pulled it from the shelf, cradling it in my palms. The front cover bore a unique symbol. A gust of wind came out of nowhere, causing the book to open in my hands. I ran my fingers over the old handwritten letters.

This journal belongest to Emily Blackstone. High priestess of the Raven Coven. Heed these words, any eyes of evil to look upon this book, will receive a painful death. Read at thy own risk.

The discovery sent a shiver down my spine. I knew I had stumbled upon something significant, something that might hold the answers I had been searching for.

Chapter 11

Nicholas

Sleep. Why can I not sleep? My eyes stared at the scuffed ceiling. I rolled onto my side; a quick squeak protested. The wall wasn't any better. People had carved all sorts of things into the concrete, and the initials were the nicest.

A loud clanging noise startled me. The sheriff stood there, smiling as the silver bars squeaked open. "Mornin', sunshine. I hope you had a wonderful stay at the Precinct Hotel. It's checkout time," he said, extending his arm. I got up quickly.

"Did you find my Emily?" I asked, heading toward the front door. The sheriff sighed, looking softer than he had the night before.

"No. But I did find out where she was buried."

The word 'buried' burned my ears. I hadn't considered that possibility. If I was alive, so was she. My eyes watered, and I turned away. I noticed a woman at the desk holding a clear container with my belongings. She pushed it towards me without looking up.

"Excuse me, where can I find the privy?" I asked. The female officer scrutinized me.

"What?" she snapped.

"Where do I urinate?" I hated using such language, but how else could I communicate? She pointed down the hall, expressionless.

I entered the privy. My reflection in the mirror caught me off guard. This man's clothes were a mess. Why place me in the body of a dirty man? I smoothed the shirt into my pants, feeling sticky jelly near my chest. My body shivered. I exited the privy and looked around. A rectangle sign read EXIT. I walked to the door and grabbed the door handle.

A bright light shined on my face, and I closed my eyes, savoring it. Air rushed into my lungs, but the warm feeling faded as clouds covered the sun. My eyes scanned the area. It felt like my hometown, but different.

"You can't just stand in front of the station. You're lucky you are even out. If Mrs. Jones had a restraint order against you, you would still be behind bars." the sheriff snapped.

"I have no place to go," I said, feeling lonely.

"There are some bed and breakfast places in town. It's about a five-minute walk through the park. Stay away from Mrs. Jones." The sheriff pointed. I nodded.

In the park, families walked around, and people ran with things in their ears. Was that how humans evolved?

A furry touch on my leg made me jump. A puppy growled low, making me smile. As I bent to pet it, my vision blurred. I was in a different time and in a younger version of my real body when a vicious dog bit my pant leg. The pain was real. I groaned, losing my balance. The dog gnawed at my ear. I swatted it away, but its teeth pierced my jaw. A high-pitched laugh echoed, pulling me out of the memory.

Suddenly, the flashback ended. I was lying on my back on the ground. The sky was bright blue. No blood. My ears were still there. The laugh drew my attention. I pulled myself up, spinning around.

"Emily?" I called, my heart racing. A woman with long, wavy brown hair made my heart skip. Emily looked so beautiful with her hair down. I placed my hand on her shoulder. "Emily."

The woman turned, eyes wide. This wasn't my Emily. The puppy pranced over and sat next to her feet. Embarrassed, I raised my hands.

"I apologize. I thought you were my wife." I quickened my pace, hearing murmurs behind me. My body started to sweat. A flash back started. I was back in time, seeing a younger boy being mocked and beaten by a male adult. The pain was mental torment. He began to expect and accept the physical pain, thinking he deserved it. A young mother helped the boy up. They connected eyes and smiled.

I gasped, returning to the present. What was going on? Why was I seeing someone else's memories? I stumbled to a bench under a beautiful oak tree. I ran to the trunk, tracing the letters, 'NB and EA'—Nicholas Blackstone and Emily Anderson. I smiled, remembering carving our names. I missed my sweet Emily.

Exhausted, I plopped onto the bench, and laid my body down. I hadn't slept well last night. A light breeze crossed my face as I closed my eyes. An image of Emily's face illuminated the back of my eyelids.

"You're not from this time, are ya?" I jolted upright, eyes landing on a young woman with blonde hair. Her necklace was a blue moon with a silver dragon. Her shirt dipped low, showing more cleavage than a respectable man felt comfortable looking at. Her brown yes sparkled.

"How did you know?" I asked, feeling a slight weight lift.

"The aura around you doesn't match the body," she replied. "You look like you have a lot on your mind. Tell me what's bothering you."

"Everything. You wouldn't understand."

"Try me." She motioned for me to follow. I took a deep breath.

"My name is Nicholas Blackstone. I was a scholar and a soldier. I came back last night into someone else's body. My wife is dead. I have no place to go. I just want my wife."

She stared ahead for a few minutes as we walked. She probably thought I was a loon.

"My great-grandmother told me stories as a child."

"I'm not making this up," I yelled.

"One story was of a witch named Emily Blackstone."

"That is my wife's name!" The words flew out of my mouth.

"I usually don't do this," she said, glancing around. "I have a spare room above my store. You can stay there until you get on your feet. My name is Violet."

As we walked into town, I marveled at the changes. Stores were everywhere now. In my day, we had only a few—a general store, an apothecary, and a tailor shop—and they were far apart.

Suddenly, a sharp pain seized my head. I clutched my skull, feeling like someone was scratching my brain. A scream of agony escaped my lips. Violet helped me to a bench. The pain intensified, and my eyes shot open. I saw the woman from last night, smiling with soft blue eyes. I had given her flowers, felt nervous, and caught a whiff of vanilla as she walked past me. Her touch sent tingles through me. Gradually, the headache subsided, and I blinked until everything became clear again.

"Well, if that wasn't eerie, I don't know what is. Your eyes turned eggshell white."

"I've been switching between this body's memories and my own since yesterday. Sometimes they combine. Dear Miss Violet, I fear I am losing my mind."

"No, you're not. What do you remember about entering this body?" Violet asked, chin on her knuckles, eyes fixed on my lips.

"I remember searching for Emily. When I found her, she and Charles were kissing," I said, voice cracking. My head started to hurt again. I grabbed Violet's arm. She screamed in pain. Everything went dark.

Suddenly, I saw Violet next to me, eyes wide with fright. She was walking backward until our eyes met.

"Nicholas, where are we?" she asked.

"Emily," Another me yelled, echoing in the air. Violet pulled me behind a boulder. We watched as my other self looked around, calling for Emily.

"Are we in one of your memories?" she whispered. I nodded.

"This was the day I died. How did you end up with me?"

"I'm a witch from Emily's coven. I didn't know ghost could pull witches into their memories like this." She said hesitantly. "Stay low. Let's follow, well, you."

We followed, hiding behind boulders. I saw Charles kissing Emily. My heart ached. I didn't want to relive this. Violet placed her hand on my back.

"Why is Emily staring blankly at you? No emotion, not even blinking," Violet noted. I watched as Charles and I clashed. His eyes turned black, blood vessel-like lines spread from his eyes, and his incisor teeth grew.

"Why didn't you tell me you died fighting the oldest vampire?" Violet exclaimed.

"Vampire..." I said, my eyes widened. "No, they can't exist. I would have read about real ones. They were always folklore... well, at least until this moment."

"Sir, you're a ghost in another man's body. Do you still need logic?" Violet's eyes pierced into me. She had a point. We watched the fight. As the other me fell, I saw something shiny in the cave's corner, Avery's amulet, but quickly returned my attention to Emily.

"This cannot be a memory. I was knocked out," I said. Emily cradled my head. Charles laughed coldly as she whispered something.

"There are no words or spells you can say to bring him back, witch. He is gone," Charles said. Anger surged through me. I wanted to fight Charles again. Emily darted to the corner, holding up her amulet yelling in a different tongue.

"No way," Violet whispered, amused. The necklace shone a bright light at Charles. He blocked it with his arms and hissed, exiting the cave. Emily collapsed. Violet and I covered our eyes as the bright light returned us to the present. The pain disappeared.

"What just happened? Did Emily die? What do you know about vampires? Why am I here? I am exhausted from all these questions and no answers," I cried. My brain was overloaded. I wanted another century-long sleep. Violet stared at the wall, then looked at me.

"I may have answers, but I need to look some stuff up. Come, let's go to my shop." She stood up hastily. I tried to keep up. We entered a small building. The smell of lavender and sage tantalized my nose.

"C'mon, Nicholas. Hurry up!" Violet yelled. I quickened my pace. Violet stopped me in front of a triangle door that was open. "This door is never open; someone is here."

Violet's fingers started to glow. Shocked, I followed her into a huge library. My heart raced with excitement at the sight of so many books. Violet's fingers had little shocks coming out, but I was too giddy to be terrified. We glanced around. No one was in sight.

"Welcome to our library. It is filled with journals of witches and other beings from the beginning of time."

"How did you retrieve all these?" I asked, gazing at the rows of books. It was the second most beautiful sight. Emily was, of course, the first. I handled the books gently, afraid to damage any of the older ones.

"You can't ruin any of these books. They've all been coated with magic," Violet informed me. "We may be witches, but we travel a lot—for fun and business. Our coven acts as historians, collecting as many books as we can. Some creatures start as friends, become enemies, then friends again. We want to know their stories, triumphs, and weaknesses. You'll have plenty of time to read them later. For now, there's only one witch we need to read about."

She walked to the back of the library. I tried to read the spines as I followed her.

"So, what witch do we need to read about?" I asked.

"Emily Blackstone of course." She said over her shoulder to me. "I have her journal right..." Suddenly, Violet gasped. My head snapped in her direction. Her hand covered her mouth, and there was a hole where a book should have been.

"No way," said a new but familiar voice. Violet and I exchanged glances and then peeked around the corner. It was the woman living in my house! She was sitting in a chair with an old book in her hand. *What was she doing here?*

"I knew you were one of us!" Violet exclaimed.

"That is the woman living in my house!" I shouted.

"That is not your house, Richard. How dare you lie like that!" The woman said, standing up quickly with a stomp.

"Okay, okay. Tensions are high right now. Let's take a breather," Violet said, walking closer to the other woman. "You're the new girl, right?"

She nodded. "Yes, I am Avery Jones. Wait, you were staring at me at the diner. Why?"

"So, you did see me then. Well, my name is Violet." She walked over and shook Avery's hand.

"Violet? My aunt talked about you a long time ago." Avery said, her blue eyes squinting at her.

Violet nodded. "She was an amazing mentor. She taught me more than I could have ever dreamed of."

"Taught you what?" Avery asked.

"Oh, that's right you don't know about us."

"Know about who?" Avery repeated. Violet lifted her finger, which glowed a bright white light. I watched as Avery hesitantly lifted her pointer finger towards Violet's. Avery took a deep breath, and then her finger glowed too! Violet lowered her arm, as Avery's eyes turned white.

"We are part of the Raven Coven," Violet stated. Avery opened her eyes and looked at us, then walked backward until her back hit the wall. She slid down, gasping for air.

"That...was...intense," Avery said slowly. Violet sat across from her and held her hand.

"You have been my best friend in so many past lives. That's why I was staring at you the other day. I hoped looking at me would spark a memory, but something held you back. Then when that disgusting vamp—" Violet's face scrunched.

"Vampire?" Avery's voice cracked.

"Yes, they are vile creatures. The one at the diner is the eldest of vampires."

"What is his name?" Avery asked, her eyes wide with concern.

"Charles. I'm surprised you didn't feel the evil radiate off him," Violet stated.

"I work with him, at the paper." Avery said slowly, her head tilted. "He kept staring at me, trying to get me to find out the truth about Nicholas Blackstone." She said, then her eyes darted back and forth between Violet and me. "Why?"

Violet and I looked at each other. She stood up and placed her hand on my shoulder.

"She needs to know."

Avery's whole body tensed, her gaze snapping to me. "No," she whispered, shaking her head. "You... you shouldn't be here. You can't be here. You're supposed to be in jail." Her voice cracked as she pressed herself tighter against the wall, arms wrapping around her knees.

I shook my head. "My name is Nicholas Blackstone. I was a scholar and a soldier. Charles killed me over a hundred years ago."

"Don't play this game with me, Richard. I don't care what tricks you're pulling." Avery said, tears formed in her eyes.

Violet crouched closer to Avery, and tried to place her hand on Avery's shoulder, but she moved it. "Avery, he's telling you the truth."

Avery stood up and paced back and forth, her eyes darting between us. I felt bad that she was so upset. "Why are you both pretending?"

Violet reached out towards Avery and gently placed her hand on Avery's shoulder. Both of their eyes went white as their bodies stayed still. I watched them both until Avery fluttered her eyes and the bright blue came back. Her chest was heaving up and down as her eyes pierced at me for a few moments. My brain was still trying to comprehend what was going on.

"Let's say I believe you. Were you the one that has been beating me all these years?" Avery asked, her arms crossed in front of her.

"Excuse me?" I was appalled. "I've seen some of the horrific things he has done to you in this body's memories. I would *never* touch a woman the way he has touched you."

Avery looked away as I walked towards her. I could see her body tense; she was a victim. I gently placed my fingers under her chin, raising her face to look at me. Her jaw clenched, lips pressed tight, but she didn't pull away.

"Look in my eyes. Are these his eyes?" I asked. For a long moment, she refused to look. Then slowly, reluctantly, her lashes lifted, and within a split second, I could not look away. I felt the room spin around the longer I looked. I felt sucked into her eyes and then into my memories. I was chasing Emily around in a field. We were laughing together and kissing gently. Everything started to spin again as I was brought back to reality.

"Did I just see your memories?" Avery exclaimed. I nodded. I did not realize she was in them as well. "What is it like to love someone so deeply like that?"

I looked down as a smile appeared on my face. "It is like getting everything you ever wanted but knowing it could be taken away in a second. We were in love during a war with a baby on the way, in a time when tomorrow was never promised."

"How are we getting him back to Emily?" Avery asked.

"We need to find my Emily's journal. We believe it has all the answers."

"You mean this book?" Avery handed me the book she had been reading. A rush of emotions took over me. Providence has finally smiled upon us.

Chapter 12

Nicholas

"Okay, so twenty-four hours ago, Nicholas, you woke up in the middle of her backyard during a storm," Violet said. My mind reeled with the weight of her words. I shook my head, struggling to piece together the fragmented memories. "Okay, Avery, what happened between you and Richard before that?"

"Richard got out of jail. He surprised me when he showed up here. I hoped he wouldn't remember how to find my aunt's house. He attacked me, right outside. I tried to run, to escape, but he caught me. I was coming to terms with the fact that he was killing me that night. And then... the lightning struck him."

We all sat in silence for a moment, thinking.

"If the lightning bolt killed Richard briefly, it would make sense that any nearby spirit could be placed inside his body. Your house isn't far from the cave," Violet explained. She walked over to a section about ghosts and spirits, pulled out a large red book, and flipped through a few pages. "Just what I thought. Since Richard technically died from the lightning, when Nicholas took over his body, it kept both their souls inside. That's why you keep seeing his memories too. We have twenty-four hours to get Richard to peacefully vacate the body, if you want to stay in his body, Nicholas. If he disagrees, well, both Richard and Nicholas's souls will go to Hell. And Nicholas, if any human body that you possess dies while your spirit is still inside, your spirit will go to hell."

I felt a rush of anxiety.

"So, you're saying if Nicholas doesn't get Richard's permission in twenty-four hours, his soul goes to Hell, and Richard dies. But if Richard agrees, Richard dies, and Nicholas gets a happily ever after?" Avery asked, sitting down heavily in a nearby chair.

"That's correct." Violet said.

I could almost feel Avery's frustration radiating from her. I was aware of the shifting tension in the room. The body I was in felt an acute, almost painful, yearning to reach out to her, to comfort her. But the anger simmering within me had to be controlled. I took a deep breath, trying to calm the storm inside. I would not lash out or raise my voice, not at her.

"Okay, so problem number two is, how do we get rid of Charles? He is the oldest vampire; he doesn't give up hunting his prey," Violet said, trying to shift the focus.

Violet looked at me, her eyes full of concern. I placed my forehead on my palms, "I still don't understand why I am his prey. We were neighbors and comrades in the military."

"Perhaps it isn't you at all," Violet said, her tone softening as she searched for another book on the bookshelf. She pulled out a black leather book and opened it, skimming through a few pages. "According to local folklore, his mother cursed him to be a vampire. She was trying to protect him from the plague and his abusive father who tormented him daily."

As Violet continued to read, her lips moving silently, I felt a deep sense of confusion and sadness. She finally looked up, her eyes glistening with tears. "I can't read this to you. I think it's better if I show you," she said, reaching for our hands.

My heart pounded as my head shot up, and then my eyes closed. Everything went dark and cold. I blinked a few times, struggling to adjust to the new sensations. Gradually, light began to seep through, and I could see Avery lying on the ground beside me. Panic surged through me as I ran over to her, carefully placing my arm under her head.

"Miss, miss, are you okay?" I asked softly, gently caressing her cheek. I didn't want to startle her. Her head stirred slightly, and she let out a groggy cough.

"Oh, thank Heavens you are alright!" I breathed a sigh of relief, feeling a rush of emotions—fear, relief, and concern. The sun beamed down on us, as it was in the center of the sky. It must have been mid-day, wherever we were.

Avery sat up, her eyes darting around in confusion. "My name is Avery, not Miss. Where are we?"

"We are in the memory of the journal I was reading," Violet explained.

"The journal has memories?" I asked, bewildered.

"No, the memory of the person who owned the journal," Violet clarified.

"Ah, that makes more sense. Who wrote this?" I asked, trying to process the surreal situation.

"Charles," Avery responded, her voice trembling. I looked at her, seeing her gaze fixed on a Charles walking angrily towards a woman in her mid-thirties.

"Are ye okay, my son?" the woman asked, her voice full of concern as she raised his face. The moonlight revealed a black eye and blood dripping from his mouth.

"Aye, mother. This was nothing compared to past beatings. I need to be better," Charles said, his voice filled with despair as he lowered his eyes.

"Nay! Don't ye ever listen to him! Ye are stronger than your father. He knows it," she insisted, her eyes fierce with determination.

"Nay! He says I am not his son!" Charles argued, his voice breaking.

"It's the ale. I promise ye, his blood runs through your veins!" She grabbed his face, their eyes locking. After a few moments, Charles began to cry and hugged his mother tightly.

Suddenly, the scene shifted. The sun started to set, casting a dusky glow over a secluded part of the woods. The woman, now alone, placed tree branches into a fire. From beneath her clothes, she pulled out an amulet with a bright blue gem set in silver, depicting a star and a half-moon. Shadows began to gather as other figures in dark, hooded cloaks appeared, their faces obscured.

"Is ye ready?" one of them asked.

"Aye. Christopher took rest. Charles is coming here," the woman replied, her voice trembling with a mix of hope and fear. "Charles will be thy savior we all prayed for. Thee will end Christopher's terror."

As the sun disappeared, the moonlight illuminated a slab of rock above the fire. The woman placed her amulet on the slab, and someone threw a dry substance into the fire, causing it to flare up higher into the air. Charles joined the others, his expression resolute.

"Mother, what may befall tonight?" he asked, his voice laced with both fear and curiosity. As he spoke, I could sense his unease, the way his eyes darted around as the others began to circle him. The fire crackled loudly, its heat radiating even from where I stood, making the night air feel thick and oppressive.

The hooded figures chanted in an unfamiliar, rhythmic tone. I watched as my heart pounded. His mother cut her palm and let a few drops of blood fall onto the amulet. She whispered something inaudible from our vantage point, her expression a mix of determination and sorrow. With a final, resolute movement, she picked up the amulet and placed it around Charles's neck.

"Mother?" he said again, his voice trembling. The moonlight caught the amulet, causing it to shine with an almost eerie brilliance. A low grunt escaped from him, turning into a pained yelp. He fell to his knees, his back arching painfully. The intensity of his screams grew louder, echoing through the night.

"My lady, they are waking from their slumber. We must hurry." One of the hooded figures urged. The chant grew louder, more insistent, with certain words emphasized in a frantic rhythm. Charles's mother joined the circle, her face a mask of grim resolve.

Charles's screams began to morph into hisses. His body contorted, his head arching backward until it aligned with the moon. His lips pulled back to reveal sharp new incisors. My stomach churned with a mix of horror and helplessness, and I tried to avert my eyes, but found myself unable to look away. I forced my eyes closed, trying to block out the grisly scene.

"I cannot watch any longer," I pleaded, my voice cracking with emotion.

"It gets worse, I'm afraid," Violet's voice was barely a whisper, her tone thick with suppressed tears.

Charles's hisses stopped, and I opened my eyes. He was staring at all the hooded figures. His mother raised her hand and the amulet glew again in the moonlight. She whispered something I couldn't understand and a circle of fire raged around the hooded figures. The beings beneath the hoods all gasped and murmured.

"Thy change will not be finished until thou hast taken of fresh blood. Each drop thou drinkest shall make thee stronger." Charles's mother's eyes lingered on him before shifting to the nearest hooded figure. "Thy sacrifice is not forgotten."

In an instant, he was behind the furthest hooded person. With a swift motion, he removed the hood, revealing a woman beneath. The rest of the hooded figures quickly followed suit, removing their hoods and chanting as they circled around him.

"It tis be cute you all believe you can stop him," his mother said with a mocking laugh. "My amulet and my blood are the only way to turn him back. Ye will never win."

One of the women, her voice filled with resolve, replied, "We shall claim that amulet. Mayhap not in this life, yet a daughter of the Raven Coven and ye bloodline shall rise to hinder him."

His mother's laughter echoed with a cold, dismissive note as Charles continued his grim work, killing each of the hooded women with a cruel efficiency. I leaned back against the boulder, feeling the weight of the situation bear down on me.

"Is this why Charles was not bothered by the blood on the battlefield?" I asked, struggling to comprehend the connection.

"Probably," Violet responded, her voice barely audible as she fought to hold back her emotions. Avery, who had been silent, came over to me, tears streaming down her face. She rested her head on my shoulder, her sobs a stark contrast to the brutal scene we had witnessed.

"Please, I don't want to be here any longer," Avery cried.

Violet nodded, closing her eyes tightly. We all woke back up in the store. Avery looked at me, her eyes wide with fear. I placed my hand gently on her shoulder, trying to offer comfort.

"Well, now we know how to stop Charles," Violet said, her voice steady but carrying an undercurrent of urgency. "We have a lot of work to prepare you, Avery."

Avery's head swiveled back and forth between me and Violet, her confusion palpable. "Preparing me for what?"

"You heard the woman," Violet said softly. "Only a witch from her bloodline can stop him. That is you."

"Me? I... I just found out I'm a witch," Avery stammered, her voice trembling with uncertainty. She began to back away, but Violet gently grabbed her hands.

"Avery, we've been best friends for many lifetimes. Please trust me. This is the first time we've had the amulet," Violet urged, her eyes filled with earnestness.

"You have the amulet?" I asked, my curiosity piqued.

Violet glanced at me and nodded. "Yes. I found it—well, let's just say borrowed it from the museum. I don't think they even realized it was missing. No one really talks much about the amulet. Some believed it's cursed. Now I know why."

Violet looked back at Avery, who was staring at the ground with a mixture of fear and resignation. She placed a comforting hand on Avery's cheek, and Avery slowly looked up at her.

"Think about all the people you'll save from someone so horrid," Violet said, her voice gentle yet firm. "If someone had stopped Richard years ago, think about how different your life would be. You have the power to save hundreds of thousands of future generations. He will remain immortal until you can stop him."

Avery's eyes stayed locked on Violet's, her expression a blend of doubt and contemplation. "Do you really think I have that kind of power?"

"I have seen your power across many lifetimes," Violet assured her, her voice filled with conviction. "With the help of the amulet and some training, I know you can!"

Avery hesitated for a moment, then hugged Violet tightly. A half-smile slowly began to form on her face. "I don't know if I have the full power that you think I do. But if you believe in me this much, I will give it a shot."

I felt a sense of determination rising within me, despite my own confusion about my place in all of this. I wasn't sure why Charles had targeted my family, but I knew I had Emily's books to uncover more answers and support Avery in any way I could.

Chapter 13

Avery

I went home, trying to understand everything that had happened. My mind whirled with the overwhelming flood of information I'd been bombarded with over the past twenty-four hours. How was it possible that I was the one chosen to confront the oldest vampire known to supernatural kind? Did the human world even know he existed? What was the truth behind his identity?

I lay in my bed, trying to sleep, but once again it tried to avoid me. I tossed and turned for hours, and after I finally dozed off, my nightmares would wake me in a cold sweat.

When my alarm clock buzzed at 7am, I turned it off and slid out of bed. My mind hazily went into routine of shower and coffee before I left for work. I was determined to avoid Charles at work as much as possible. I needed more time to process everything.

He wasn't at his desk, so I placed my headsets on my head and worked straight through the entire day. I was surprised he didn't try to force me to talk. A few times I felt the hair on the back of my neck stand up, like he had been watching me.

When my phone screen read 6 p.m. I darted out of the office and went right back to Violet's shop.

A loud bang startled me, as I opened the door. The rush of heat from the small black iron pot that Violet called her cauldron, heated my face. The acrid smell of burnt rubber filled the air, and my nose wrinkled in disgust. We had all heard of witches and their potions from TV shows, but nothing could have prepared me for this.

"What on earth are you cooking?" I asked, my voice tinged with a mix of curiosity and irritation. I waved my hand in front of my nose, trying to clear the foul smell. Violet, her face a mask of concentration, raised one finger in the air and continued to add herbs to the pot. Her muttered incantations in Latin—or what I assumed was Latin—seemed almost rhythmic.

"I'm making my famous protection potion," Violet explained, her voice steady but her eyes never leaving the pot. A silver spoon hovered above the cauldron, stirring the thick, shimmering liquid all on its own. "It needs to stir for several hours while it simmers. The spell keeps it moving, but it still needs someone to watch in case it bubbles over or thickens too fast."

She turned toward Nicholas, who had been silently observing from the corner. "Nicholas, would you mind keeping an eye on it? If the color shifts too dark or it starts to smoke, call for me."

Nicholas nodded solemnly. "Of course. I'll stay close and maybe read some of those books while I'm at it," he added with a faint smile, glancing toward the nearby stack of ancient tomes.

Our eyes met for a moment, his brown eyes a shade lighter than normal, and I couldn't help but think how strange it was that another man's mind was controlling Richard's body. His smile was softer than Richard's ever had been. I returned it weakly before hurrying to catch up with Violet, who was already heading toward the back wall of the library.

Violet stood before an empty wall, her arms outstretched, her eyes closed in concentration. I marveled at how she used her arms so expressively in her spells. It amazed me that her physical strength didn't seem to match the intensity of her magic.

She began mumbling in Latin again. As the gold circle began to form on the wall, swirling with intricate loops and patterns, I couldn't help but wonder how much bigger this place could get. The crackling noise grew louder, and the wall slowly extended into a new room.

Violet lowered her arms with a satisfied smile. "This is the safest room in town. The Raven Coven placed a powerful protection spell on it, along with a protective border around the entire building."

"Wait, is there something like this around my home? Charles made me say in specific words that he could come in my home." I said, my mind racing with that memory.

"Yes," Violet confirmed. "Your aunt was so important to us that we couldn't allow her home to be unprotected."

I took a moment to reflect on this. The thought of my aunt being vulnerable or not as invincible as I had always believed was unsettling. I wish I hadn't stayed away the last ten years. Maybe she would have shared this hidden world with me. *Why hadn't she?*

"Thank you for caring for her when I wasn't around," I said, my voice softening with gratitude. Violet took my hands in hers, her eyes glistening with warmth.

"She would be so proud of you," she said, her voice tender. She squeezed my hands gently before letting go. "Now, let's get started. There's much to learn about our heritage."

"I'm ready," I insisted, trying to shake off the lingering doubts. In the center of the room was a massive, projected family tree. It shimmered with gold specks floating around it.

"This is our family tree," Violet said, her voice filled with reverence. "It's more majestic than any oak. We have many branches, but a strong core. The Raven Coven believes that when we pass, we enter the witch's realm. We can communicate with our ancestors there whenever we wish."

As the gold specks combined into a ray of light that danced around me, I felt an unprecedented calmness wash over me. I moved slightly, following the way the light twirled like it had a will of its own. The sensation was soothing—otherworldly. "I can feel her," I whispered, my voice thick with emotion. Tears pressed at the corners of my eyes as the ray returned to the tree, dissolving into a thousand golden motes. My breaths, which had been shallow, steadied. I let out a soft laugh.

Violet smiled knowingly. "What you're feeling is the connection between you and every witch who came before. This tree holds the memory of our line—their souls, their lessons, their power. Watch closely."

The golden specks shimmered and reformed across the branches, illuminating countless leaves. Some flickered faintly, like distant stars; others glowed brighter, alive with warmth. As I gazed closer, I swore I saw shapes within them—faces of women I didn't know but somehow recognized. A healer draped in moonlight. A warrior gripping a staff of fire. A scholar surrounded by ancient runes. And a girl kneeling before a pentagram, just as I had.

"Those are your past lives," Violet whispered. "Each leaf is a soul reborn—a life lived, a lesson learned, a strength passed on. You carry them all within you, Avery. Every one of them still breathes through your spirit."

A lump formed in my throat. The air hummed faintly around us, as if the women in the tree were whispering my name.

"At the far edge of the tree, in the shadowy area, is Charles's mother's branch," Violet explained, her tone shifting, pointing to the darker section where the leaves glowed dimly. "She had one more child after Charles was turned into a vampire. Charles was not pleased—he feared his father's anger would fall on the boy too. But his father adored the child, and that bloodline continued."

Violet moved toward a brighter section, where the leaves shimmered like morning sunlight. "And here is Emily."

"Emily—Nicholas's wife?" I asked, my mind spinning. Violet nodded solemnly.

"The unsettling part," she said, her tone heavy, "is that Charles impregnated Emily years later. You are a descendant of Emily, but not Nicholas, because you come from that child."

I blinked, trying to process it all. Part of me was relieved that I wasn't connected by blood to Nicholas—especially considering the body he now inhabited. The thought made my stomach twist.

"We're not entirely sure how he managed it," Violet continued. "Rumor says he used his compulsion on a witch from another coven, forcing her to brew an enchanted potion with her blood and his. Under the blood moon, the mixture gave him power to overcome vervain—and bend even a witch to his will."

My hand trembled slightly. "Where do my aunt and I fit into all of this?"

Violet smiled softly and guided my hand to a lower branch of the tree. The leaves there shimmered, their edges outlined in radiant gold. "You're right there," she said with pride. "You're the new leaf—the continuation of every soul that came before. The one who can change everything."

As I stared, a single leaf at the tip of the branch began to glow brighter than the rest. Its light pulsed in rhythm with my heartbeat. For a fleeting second, I saw reflections of my past selves within it—the healer, the warrior, the scholar—all merging into one radiant form. Me.

The weight of it all pressed into my chest, a mixture of awe and fear. A family of heroes and villains, of love and betrayal—and now me. A woman who'd once been broken, who'd only recently found the courage to rise.

A speck of gold drifted from the glowing leaf, spiraling downward until it touched my cheek. Warmth spread through me instantly, wrapping around my heart like sunlight breaking through fog. The calmness returned—stronger this time, anchored deep within.

"How could I possibly confront the eldest vampire? I wasn't even strong enough to leave an abusive relationship."

Violet must have seen the turmoil on my face because she walked over to me and gently raised my chin. Her fingers were soft and reassuring as she wiped away the tears streaming down my face. "That doesn't mean you're weak. It takes strength to survive something like that and not give up in the world. That's strength."

I could hardly respond through my sobs, but her words struck a chord deep within me. I clung to her, burying my face in her shoulder as I cried. The support from someone who understood my pain was a comfort I hadn't realized I needed. After a few moments, Violet patted my back gently.

"Are you ready to kick some vamp ass?" she asked with a teasing note in her voice. Was I really ready for this? The word 'destiny' sounded heroic in stories, but in real life, it felt heavy.

I wiped my tears away, feeling a surge of determination. "Hell yes," I said, my voice stronger now. Violet's smile widened in approval. She moved over to another part of the room, where a huge pentagram was etched into the floor. The intricate design seemed to pulse with energy. Violet sat down in the center of the pentagram, her posture relaxed but purposeful.

"This pentagram represents the elements—Earth, Air, Fire, Water, and Spirit," Violet began, her tone calm but deliberate.

"It helps us maintain harmony with the universe and protects us from outside influences. I want you to sit crisscrossed here and close your eyes."

"Like this?" I asked, adjusting my legs beneath me.

"Exactly," Violet confirmed. "Now, breathe in through your nose, out through your mouth. Again. Slower. I want you to clear your mind. Let go of every worry. Just focus on the feeling of peace."

That was easier said than done. My thoughts darted like startled birds–images of Charles's haunting eyes, the weight of being told I was a witch, and the terrifying notion that I was supposed to stop an ancient vampire. My pulse quickened despite the quiet room around me.

"Focus," Violet whispered. "Find something simple to anchor yourself to. A sound, a scent, or a feeling. Let it lead you to calm."

I took another breath. And another. Slowly, the candlelight behind my eyelids began to dim into something else. I could almost hear the low hum of computers, the clatter of keyboards, and the faint click of heels echoing across a newsroom floor. The smell of ink, toner, and stale coffee wrapped around me. It was oddly comforting–the scent of purpose, of routine, and of stories waiting to be told.

That place had always grounded me. Even on the worst days, the newsroom's chaos had a rhythm, one I could move to. For a moment, I imagined myself there again–pen in hand, notebook open, and my heart steady. The noise faded into focus, and peace settled where panic had been.

"Good," Violet's voice echoed softly. "You've found it. Remember how this feels. This is your sanctuary. When fear threatens to consume you, close your eyes and breathe. Call this feeling back, and it will return."

The scent of coffee and ink faded, replaced by the quiet stillness of Violet's room. I opened my eyes to see her warm smile. There was something grounding about the way Violet carried herself. Even when the air shimmered with magic, Violet felt solid. The candles flickered gently, their light reflected in the curve of the pentagram.

"Okay, now for some defensive magic," Violet said, her enthusiasm palpable. "What do you know about vampires?"

"They don't like garlic or sunlight, unless they're like the Cullens, who sparkle in the sun," I blurted out, feeling a little embarrassed by my pop culture knowledge.

Violet laughed softly. "Ha, well, that's more fiction than fact. Real vampires can endure brief sunlight—just enough to move from one shadow to the next. Most burn within seconds, but some... have found ways around that."

I tilted my head. "Like Charles?"

Her expression darkened slightly. "Exactly. Charles wears a daylight ring—an artifact enchanted by a witch centuries ago to protect him from the sun's full force. The stone is infused with an elemental spell that bends light around him, making it appear as though he's unaffected. But it's temporary protection. The spell requires constant balance. If too much light touches him—pure, unfiltered sunlight—it can still burn through the enchantment."

My eyes widened. "So that's why he can walk around during the day."

"Yes," Violet said, nodding. "The witch who created it was from the Hallowmere Coven. Their records are some of the oldest our line ever preserved. I've studied them for years." She gestured toward her shelves of grimoires and weathered scrolls. "That's how I learned the specifics of the spell—how it draws energy from the sun itself, turning a weakness into a shield."

I swallowed. "And the sun shield spell you're about to teach me—how does that fit in?"

"Ah," she said, eyes glinting with purpose. "The light barrier you'll cast creates a *natural* halo of sunlight energy—pure, unfiltered. If Charles steps too close, it'll disrupt the enchantment in his ring. The magic will cancel out, and the sun will hit him directly."

"So it would hurt him."

"Painfully," Violet confirmed. "But only if your shield is strong enough. That's why you must focus. Think of it as drawing sunlight inward, letting it pulse out from you rather than burn you. Ready to try?"

I nodded, feeling a mix of apprehension and determination.

"Good. Stand with your feet shoulder-width apart, palms open. Focus on the light around you, not the shadows," Violet said.

I drew in a steady breath, fixing my eyes on a faint line in the wall. "Lumen protegat me, hostes excludat," I recited, repeating the incantation.

A faint warmth flickered around my fingertips, like sunlight breaking through clouds.

A warmth began at my toes and spread throughout my body, reaching the top of my head. I cracked open one eye to see Violet's face lit up with excitement. Her jumping and clapping filled me with a sense of accomplishment.

"Alright," Violet said, catching her breath. "Before we dive into more spells, I want you to look at your aunt's spell book. I'm going to retrieve the amulet while you familiarize yourself with it." She handed me a large, brown leather book with gold latches and trim. The gold pentagram on the cover gleamed subtly.

As I flipped through the pages, I saw my aunt's handwritten notes filling the margins. Each note was a glimpse into her world, her thoughts. When I reached the last page, a note addressed to me caught my eye:

Avery,

I wanted to tell you about our coven. Your mother swore me to secrecy. If you are reading this, your destiny is already coming to fruition. I know the Raven Coven will teach you everything you need to know. Remember, no matter how dark it may be, I will be there to light your way.

Love,

Auntie.

A tear slipped from my eye as I read her words. I looked up to see Violet standing in front of me, her eyes scanning the room with a troubled expression.

"Violet, what's wrong?" I asked, my heart sinking.

"The amulet," Violet said, her voice tinged with alarm. "It's gone."

Chapter 14

Avery

Violet led me down a narrow hallway, the flickering candlelight casting eerie shadows on the stone walls. After a week of lessons with Violet, I should be used to her having rooms upon rooms in this small building, but I wasn't quite there yet.

"There's something I want to show you," Violet said, her voice hushed yet filled with purpose. I followed her, my curiosity piqued. We stopped in front of a heavy wooden door. Violet pushed it open, revealing a room that seemed frozen in time. Shelves lined the walls with magical weapons and artifacts. Swords with glowing runes, daggers with jeweled hilts, and staffs that seemed to hum with power all filled the room. The air was thick with the scent of metal and leather, a combination that felt oddly empowering.

"This was your aunt's armory," Violet explained. "She spent countless hours here, not just practicing spells, but also preparing for any supernatural threat. I thought it might help you connect with her magic."

Violet placed her hand on my shoulder, smiled, and followed me while I stepped inside. I felt a sense of reverence wash over me, as I watched Violet walk towards a rack of swords, giving me space. My fingers trailed over the weapons hanging on the nearby wall, the cool metal and smooth wood comforting. It was like stepping into a part of her world, a place where her presence still lingered.

I opened my aunt's book; my fingers enjoyed the feel of the old pages. The rough, aged texture was comforting, even though in this lifetime, I was touching it for the first time. The smell of old parchment and ink filled the air, bringing an odd sense of familiarity. My eyes moved side to side as I read every word, my mind absorbing the unfamiliar Latin with surprising ease. It was as if muscle memory from a past life guided me.

"Stake shield. Use this spell to conjure a barrier made from stakes to impale any vampire, except the eldest. It will only weaken him for moments. He is immortal."

I gulped hard. The word "immortal" sent shivers up my spine, a cold dread settling in my stomach. What if we couldn't defeat him? Would I be running from him my entire life?

Violet noticed my apprehension and placed a comforting hand on my shoulder. "Why don't you try the stake shield spell? It's better to practice now while we're safe."

I nodded, taking a deep breath to steady myself. I positioned myself in the center of the room and began chanting the incantation. The words felt foreign yet familiar on my tongue, the power of the spell building with me.

Suddenly, sharp wooden stakes materialized around me, hovering menacingly. I directed them forward, but my control wavered, and they shot towards Violet. My heart lurched in fear.

Violet's eyes widened, but she remained calm. With a swift motion, she waved her hand, redirecting the stakes to embed themselves harmlessly into the wall beside her. I stared in shock, my breath coming in quick gasps.

"I'm so sorry, Violet!" I exclaimed, my voice trembling.

She smiled reassuringly. "It's okay, Avery. It takes time to master these spells. Your aunt told me she struggled when she first learned, and so did I. The important thing is that you keep practicing."

I nodded, still shaken but determined. The experience had taught me the importance of control and precision in wielding magic. I would need to be better if we were to stand a chance against our enemies. Nicholas's head peaked into the room.

"I heard a loud bang. Are you two alright?" He asked. Violet nodded, then looked back at me. I watched as Nicholas's mouth gaped as he looked around the armory.

"Avery, you can help me with a tracking spell," Violet stated, pulling me from my thoughts. I looked over at her, my eyes wide and unblinking. Fear gripped my heart and mind again, making my breaths shallow.

"What if we can't locate this amulet? Will I have to hide from him forever?" My voice trembled, betraying the terror that gnawed at me.

"No. He doesn't even know that you are the one to turn him," Nicholas stated as he entered the room, obviously having overheard my worry. He turned to Violet, "Wait, does he?"

Violet paced back and forth, shaking her head, "How am I supposed to know? I am a witch, not a mind reader." Her frustration was evident in the tightness of her movements and the sharpness of her words.

"Wait, you can't hear inside other's minds?" I asked, shocked. Violet's eyebrow raised as she shook her head.

"That would be a useful tool right now, though," Nicholas chimed in, trying to lighten the mood. Violet and I both looked at him, our expressions stern.

"Did you find anything useful in Emily's book?" I asked, trying to refocus my mind and suppress the rising panic.

"Possibly. According to Emily's journal, she signed a treaty with all the supernatural beings in the community." Nicholas's voice was steady, a stark contrast to the turmoil inside me.

"Wait. What other supernatural beings?" I asked, my curiosity momentarily overriding my fear.

"Werewolves. Elves. Other vampires, although they are sired by Charles. Then there are sirens in the water. And something called shapeshifters." Nicholas listed them off, his tone scholarly and detached.

Violet looked at me, her eyes drawn to the book in my hands. Her finger moved rhythmically, a smile spreading across her face as if she had just solved a puzzle.

"Okay, we need to locate this amulet. Then, I can go talk to the other supernatural beings. They are not keen on strangers," Violet spoke quickly, her body tensing as if preparing for battle.

"Wait, so you knew about the treaty?" Nicholas questioned. Violet nodded.

"Of course I did. I know everything from most of these books in this library. I have interacted with almost every family of supernaturals here. This is my home. We just try to stay away from each other to not cause any stirs with Charles. However, the time has come to make him stir."

Violet walked to a map on the counter and motioned for me to join her. She had a quartz crystal tied to a piece of string, its surface gleaming under the dim light.

"This is called a pendulum. We will ask it to locate the amulet."

"Sounds simple," I said. Violet stared at me; one eyebrow raised in skepticism. "Sorry, I didn't mean it like that."

Violet held the string above the map. I watched with hope that we would be able to locate the amulet.

"This is exhilarating! I once read a story about a coven using this to find missing children. The townspeople blamed the coven for their disappearance. The mayor agreed to stop blaming them if they used their magic to locate the children safely." Nicholas recounted, his voice filled with a mix of awe and nervous energy.

"We seek out the amulet of Elenor. Please show us its current location." The pendulum began to move in larger circles, the crystal swinging with increasing intensity. Violet's wrist remained steady as her arm moved over different sections of the map until the pendulum dropped, landing on a specific house on Harrowgate Avenue.

"This is what I feared," Violet said, slowly lowering herself into a nearby chair, her shoulders slumping as if the weight of the world had settled on them. "Charles took it."

My stomach dropped. "How did he take it? I thought he couldn't even step foot past the barrier."

"He can't," Violet confirmed, her tone sharp. "The wards were crafted to repel the undead and any creature corrupted by dark magic. They recognize intent and energy—if something is unnatural, it's pushed back."

"However," Nicholas interjected, "they don't recognize *borrowed intent.*"

Violet looked up, grimly nodding. "If Charles used his compulsion on a normal human—someone with no supernatural essence—the wards wouldn't see the threat. They'd see only an innocent soul entering freely. The magic protects against monsters, not the manipulated."

I frowned. "So, he sent someone else in for him."

"Exactly," Violet said bitterly. "A human puppet. The wards can't differentiate between will and influence. That's their weakness—and he exploited it."

Nicholas leaned back with a wry smile. "A loophole in magic. Both exciting and absurd."

We both turned to look at him. He raised his hands. "What? I'm a scholar. I take an unhealthy interest in loopholes and contracts."

His attempt at humor earned no laughs. The gravity of the situation pressed heavily in the air.

I walked over to another chair nearby, the creak of the old wood breaking the silence. Violet stared at the floor, her lips pressed into a thin line, her brows furrowed in deep thought.

"I failed our coven. I failed the world." Her voice was a whisper, heavy with guilt.

"No, you failed no one," Nicholas said, placing a comforting hand on Violet's shoulder. "Yes, we have a bump in the road. But there are three intelligent individuals here. Together, we will figure out how to get the amulet back."

"He is right. This is no longer just on you. We will use our smarts to make a plan," I said, offering a half-smile to Violet. But how do we get past a vampire, I wondered.

"We need a distraction. Perhaps if I tell him I am Nicholas, that will get him out of the house," Nicholas suggested.

"But he could decide he wants to kill you again. That would do none of us any good," Violet said.

"But I really serve little purpose here. Let me help fight."

"You serve more purpose than to die," I said, standing up, feeling a surge of determination. "You helped open my eyes to another world. Both of you did. One I never dreamed possible."

I felt a strange mix of gratitude and fear. The reality of our situation was sinking in, but I knew I wasn't alone.

"We need a different plan. None of us are dying," Violet said firmly, her eyes narrowing with determination. My gaze wandered back to the ancient book in my hands, the pages filled with my aunt's meticulous handwriting. *Come on, auntie, what would you do?* I thought to myself, searching for inspiration.

"Why don't we case his house?" I suggested, the idea forming as I spoke.

"What exactly does that mean?" Nicholas questioned, his brow furrowed.

"Sorry, why don't we go to his house and watch who comes in and out? Learn the ins and outs of his day," I clarified, hoping they would understand the importance of surveillance.

"Wouldn't he see us?" Nicholas asked, doubt creeping into his voice.

"Not when you have some powerful witches on your side," Violet interjected with a sly smile. "I'll make some calls to the woman in our coven, see if they can help us with some invisibility spells."

I nodded, feeling a surge of relief that she took the reigns of my idea. I wasn't sure of any more than the idea. Violet pulled out her phone, her fingers moving swiftly as she typed out a message, and my mind raced. Would the coven respond quickly enough? Could we truly pull this off without being detected? Within minutes, responses started pouring in.

The next evening, the living room was filled with the soft murmurs of arriving witches, their presence bringing a comforting sense of security. Each one carried the unique aura of their magic, a testament to their individual strengths. We gathered around the coffee table, our voices low but filled with purpose.

Violet grabbed my hand, guiding me over to a seasoned witch with silver streaks in her hair. Violet placed a hand on her shoulder. "Avery, this is Luna. She's one of our strongest witches and a close friend. Luna, this is Avery."

Luna's eyes softened as she looked at me. "I'm so sorry about your aunt. We grew up together. She was a wonderful woman and a powerful witch. She would be proud of you."

Her words hit me harder than I expected, a mixture of sorrow and pride swelling within me. "Thank you, Luna." I said, my voice barely above a whisper.

"We'll need to form a circle around the car," Luna instructed, turning to the task at hand. "The spell requires our combined energy to maintain the invisibility."

As we stepped outside, the cool night air brushed against my skin, heightening my senses. We positioned ourselves around my car, our hands linked to form an unbroken chain. I glanced at Nicholas, his eyes wide with a mix of awe and apprehension. Neither one of us had seen magic from a coven done before. Luna walked over to me, grabbing one of my hands while grabbing another witch's hand.

"Close your eyes and focus on the car," Luna's voice was calm, guiding us into the spell. I took a deep breath, centering my thoughts on the vehicle. I could feel the energy building around us, a palpable force that connected each of us.

"Magic is as much about intent as it is about power," Violet said on the other side of me. I poured my intent into the spell, imagining the car fading from sight, blending seamlessly with the surroundings.

A soft hum filled the air, growing louder as the spell took hold. The energy pulsed through me, a warm, comforting sensation. I opened my eyes just in time to see the car shimmer and then disappear. A collective sigh of relief passed through the circle.

"It's done," Luna said, her voice tinged with satisfaction. "The car is hidden."

Nicholas and I climbed into the now-invisible car, careful not to disrupt the spell. The seats felt cool beneath me, a stark contrast to the adrenaline coursing through my veins. As we settled in, I couldn't help but feel a strange sense of pride. We were doing this—we were taking control of our fate.

"Nicholas, when we get there, keep an eye on the front door," I instructed, my voice steady. "I'll watch the side entrance and the back." Nicholas nodded his head.

Chapter 15

Nicholas

As I sat in Avery's car, the tension of the watch weighed heavily on me. Charles's house loomed in the distance, its shadow casting a foreboding presence. My mind drifted, and suddenly, I was asleep.

"Please, you don't have to do this." A female's voice echoed in my ears. Slowly, I opened my eyes to find Avery with crimson streaks rolling down her face, her eyes wide and filled with fear. My chest and ears pounded as I looked down at my hand, gripping a silver blade with a dragon on the handle. The dragon's blue eyes reflected Avery's tears. I wanted to throw the knife away, but I had no control over my actions. A male's voice came from me, but it wasn't me.

"Bitch, get on your knees like I told you," The voice demanded, followed by a slap to Avery's face. Inside, I screamed, but my body didn't respond. I could only watch as he pushed her down on all fours, yanking a fistful of her hair while he used the hand with the knife to unsnap his pants. Desperation consumed me; I wanted to make him suffer, to drive the dragon's tongue through his appendage. The thought made me cringe, but what he was doing to Avery was so much worse. Her screams and sobs filled the room as he violated her repeatedly.

"Now look back at me and show me those mesmerizing eyes of yours," the voice demanded. Avery's tear-streaked face turned, her beautiful blue eyes now cold as ice, eyeliner smeared. The sight of her suffering was unbearable.

"Nicholas?" Avery's voice pulled me out of my nightmare. I blinked and looked into her concerned blue eyes; her brows furrowed with worry. I hugged her tightly, my body shaking. "Nicholas, you're shaking. What is wrong?"

"I don't know what I saw," I replied, sinking back into the car seat. Avery held my hands, her touch grounding me. "I tried to stop it, but I had no control. There was a dragon knife—" Avery's hands squeezed mine, a tear rolling down her cheek. "Avery, what happened?"

"That wasn't a dream," she said softly, her voice distant as she stared straight ahead, lost in the memory. "It was supposed to be a fun day. The sun was beating down on us, but a slight breeze shielded us from the heat. My work had a small barbecue. It was always a great time until Richard passed his alcohol tolerance. He would start getting handsy. I didn't like that in front of co-workers. He wanted to go home so we could be alone. The moment we slid into the cab, Richard grabbed me and kissed me hard. His hand yanked at my dress until it slipped low on my chest, leaving my bra and the tops of my breasts exposed. I kept asking him to stop, but he wouldn't. The cab driver's old eyes watched in the mirror, dark and open wide, anxious to see what I had under my dress. Richard slid his hand under my dress and his finger entered me. It felt great, but I didn't want it right there. When the cab pulled up, I rushed to the front door, embarrassed. My mind was spinning all over the place. I was mad he wouldn't listen. I was angry he drank himself to that point. I felt like an object too. Like he did not care if someone else could see us—well, me—naked. I sat on the toilet and cried. Richard banged on the door trying to get in. The locked door made him angrier. I didn't care though. I felt safer in there. I told him to go to bed and sleep off the alcohol, that this was not him. It was quiet on the other side for a few minutes. I was able to collect my thoughts and just looked at my face in the mirror. I splashed cold water on my face. I wiped the smeared eyeliner off. Suddenly, I watched him break down the door. His eyes were dark and sinister, like he knew he was getting what he wanted. His lips curled up in a smirk as he raised his hand with the dragon knife. I knew I was in trouble. I was helpless. The worst part, that dragon knife was what my father gave him before he died. He always wanted to pass it on to a man he looked at as a son. No matter how much I begged, no matter how much I screamed, he would not stop. Towards the end, I gave up. I blanked my mind. Next thing I remembered was waking up in the hospital. My sister had found me the next day bleeding and passed out on the floor. Richard was passed out on the bed."

"That is horrible. I am sorry he put you through that," I said, my voice trembling with emotion. I squeezed her hands, wanting to take away some of her pain.

"You remind me a lot of how he used to be, when we first met. I wish we had the love you and Emily have. I truly want to help you find out the truth and stop Charles," Avery said with a glimmer of hope in her eyes. Her determination was contagious, and I felt a renewed sense of purpose. Together, we would stop Charles, no matter the cost.

"Emily and I...we've been through a lot," I replied, my voice barely above a whisper. "I understand the hardships of a relationship."

For a moment, we sat in silence, a rare moment of peace during the chaos. I clung to it.

Suddenly, a movement caught my eye. Near Charles's house, still some distance away, a figure detached itself from the shadows. Tall and lean, he moved with an eerie, fluid grace that made the hair on my arms stand up.

Before I could process what I was seeing, he was no longer by the house. In the blink of an eye, he was gliding across the yard with unnatural speed, his head lifting slightly as if tasting the air. Within seconds, he was only a few feet from the car.

My heart skipped a beat as realization struck: a vampire.

The vampire paused, sniffing the air, his eyes narrowing as he scanned the area. "I can smell people nearby," he said, his voice a low growl. He was just a few feet away from our car, and I held my breath, praying he wouldn't notice us.

Avery tensed beside me, her grip on my hand tightening. We couldn't just sneak in. Not with a vampire guarding the place.

The vampire continued to sniff the air, his gaze sweeping the area. "I know you're out there," he called, his voice carrying a dangerous edge. "You can't hide from me."

Just then, a noise came from the woods behind the vampire. He turned, his senses heightened. A deer stepped out of the underbrush, its eyes wide with fear. The vampire licked his lips, his predatory instincts taking over, and darted off after the deer with blinding speed.

"Now," Avery whispered urgently. She started the car as quietly as she could, the engine's low hum blending into the night. We pulled away, our hearts still racing from the close call.

"We'll need a new plan," Avery said, her voice steady despite the tension.

"Yeah," I agreed, my mind racing with possibilities. "And we'll need to be careful. Very careful."

The night was far from over, and the stakes were higher than ever.

Avery

We watched Charles's house every night for a week. We watched who came in, how many vampires guarded the house, and any thing we thought could be imperative.

Nicholas and I burst into Violet's shop the morning after our last steak out, frustration etched on our faces. Violet looked up from her work, her eyes widening slightly at the sight of us.

"That good, huh?" she remarked, setting aside the herb she had been sorting.

I sighed, sinking into a chair. "We can't get close to the house without being detected. That vampire Adrian is always guarding it."

Nicholas nodded, his jaw tight with tension. "We almost got caught by him last week. If it wasn't for that deer distracting him, we'd be toast."

Violet's expression turned serious. "We need a new approach."

We sat in silence for a few moments, each of us lost in our thoughts. Doubt began to creep in, a heavy weight pressing down on my chest. What if we were always one step behind Charles?

A sudden idea sparked in my mind, breaking through the haze of doubt. "What if I called Charles and told him he was right? That I need his help with this Nicholas Blackstone article. I could ask to discuss it over dinner at his house."

Nicholas scoffed immediately, his protective nature flaring. "You are not going to that predator's house alone."

"You're right, I'm not."

"Good," he said, looking at me confused.

"You're going with me."

"What?" Nicholas sharply asked.

"You can enter his basement and look around the house for me. He will never expect you since he doesn't know about you! And Adrian will be busy checking me out!"

"That is true. It is crazy enough, it might work," Violet said, her eyes lighting up with a glimmer of hope.

I smiled at Violet; glad she was on my side. I looked at Nicholas. "So, you in? I understand if you're scared," I boasted. "Richard was a coward too."

Nicholas bristled, his eyes narrowing. "I beg your pardon! A person can be scared without being a coward! It is normal to be scared going against a predator. Besides, I am not afraid to die."

"Then what *are* you afraid of?" I asked. I walked over to him and grabbed his hand. His eyes looked up at me, filled with a mix of sorrow and resolve.

"This body and I are concerned about what Charles will do to you if he finds out. I already lost my life and my wife to him. I do not intend to lose you." I hugged him when he said that, feeling a warmth spread through me. Knowing I was cared about by both Nicholas and Richard made me feel oddly better.

"Okay, now let me call Charles." I scrolled through my phone, looking for his name. I had barely touched the green call button when he picked it up–it only rang once.

"Hello?" Charles's voice questioned.

"Hi Charles. It's Avery."

"Yeah, my caller ID told me that. What's up?"

"Well, I wanted to apologize for my behavior lately. There is a lot that you do not know about me. But you were right about one thing," I said hesitantly, my heart pounding in my chest.

"What's that?"

"I do want to make a name for myself. I thought doing it on my own would be best, but..." my voice trailed off, hoping my uncertainty sounded genuine.

"I would love to help you, Avery. Why don't you come by my house tonight? I can make you dinner while we talk about your past that I don't know about."

"And Nicholas Blackstone, right? My article is due tomorrow morning."

"Give me about an hour. I'll send you the address," he said, his tone turning slightly eager.

"Perfect. Thank you again, Charles. I really do appreciate this." I hung up the phone. Violet and Nicholas stared at me for a few seconds. "What?"

"That higher-pitched tone you used. Intriguing," Nicholas stated. He walked away towards the library.

"Where are you going?" Violet yelled out. Nicholas turned around, his expression resolute.

"If we are going to sneak into Charle's home, I want to know as much about him as possible. I will read over Emily's journal again and see if any of these books have the layout of his home. I know a few books had the layout of my home."

"If there is a blueprint of his home, we could use the location spell again to find out exactly where the amulet is," Violet suggested. Nicholas bowed slightly to Violet, then turned back to the library.

That is a smart idea. I thought, feeling a flicker of hope. Violet was still sitting in the chair; her face no longer looked despaired, but her eyes were wide with unease.

"We need to finish getting you ready for tonight, just in case things do not go as planned. Vampires on their own can be tricky. Charles has had hundreds of years to perfect manipulation." Her voice was steady, but I could see the worry in her eyes. "We need to also have some weapons on you. Small enough to do damage, but not big enough for him to see it."

The next thirty minutes went quickly. Violet taught me how to file down the edge of wood to make a stake, her hands steady and confident as she worked. We also performed a spell to enchant the stake. She said this would make it stronger to penetrate Charles's hard skin. It wouldn't kill him, but it would stop him. Once he is human, that would kill him.

I wore a pair of black jeans and a three-quarter sleeve shirt. The shoulders had holes, showing my skin. It was black and had a skull on it. I wore a leather jacket over it. It had a pocket on the inside long enough to hold the stake and a few other magical items. I wore my hair down and applied some make-up: white eye shadow to make my eyes look more awake, and some eye liner and mascara. I looked at myself in a full-length mirror at Violet's shop. My reflection stared back at me, a mixture of fear and determination in my eyes.

"You are positive the stake is not noticeable?" I questioned Violet, turning to face her.

"I am positive." Violet placed her arms on my shoulders, giving them a reassuring squeeze. Nicholas walked into the room, his eyes widening slightly as a gasp of air exited his mouth.

"Oh wow. You look stunning," Nicholas added, his voice tinged with admiration. I smiled, feeling a blush creep up my cheeks.

"Thank you. I hope Charles is distracted enough."

"You would distract the devil himself," Nicholas said. I could feel my cheeks heat further, the warmth spreading across my face.

"Let's go." I said, my voice steady despite the butterflies in my stomach. As we walked out, the weight of the mission ahead of us pressed down on me heavily, but the connection between us had grown stronger. Nicholas and I were no longer enemies turned allies; we were partners in this fight against the darkness.

The night was approaching, and soon it would be time to put our plan into action. My heart pounded with a mix of fear and determination. There was no turning back now.

Chapter 16

Nicholas

My mind was all over the place. This was only the third time I had ever been inside a motor vehicle, and the sensation was still alien to me. The first time I was in the back seat of the sheriff's vehicle, the second time in an invisible car, and now I could actually see all of the knobs and lights of the interior controls Avery had explained to me. Avery was driving faster than the law enforcement officer, and the speed only added to my disorientation.

I fidgeted in my seat, trying to get comfortable. My fingers found the buttons for the window, and I watched with a mix of fascination and trepidation as the glass slid up and down. I did it a few times, just to feel the strange, smooth motion. The cool breeze that entered when the window was down helped clear my mind a bit, though the noise of the wind rushing past made it hard to think.

Next, I played with the air conditioning vents, angling them in different directions and adjusting the airflow. The cool air felt good against my face, a stark contrast to the oppressive heat outside. I marveled at the technology, so different from anything I had known in my previous life.

I glanced over at her a few times, trying to gauge her state of mind. Her focus on the road was intense, her eyes darting occasionally to the rearview mirror. I wanted to show I had no doubts that Avery would keep Charles distracted, but to be frank, she was distracting this body as well. She looked absolutely stunning, and I couldn't help but feel a pang of jealousy, knowing she would be in close quarters with the man who had kissed my wife before I died.

Avery caught me fiddling with the dashboard controls and smiled slightly. "Having fun?"

"Just trying to get a feel for things," I replied, managing a weak smile. "This is all still so new to me."

She nodded, her expression softening. "I get it. Just hang tight. We're almost there."

I took a deep breath and tried to steady my nerves. The dashboard's lights and gauges were a mesmerizing array of information, and I found myself lost in the details. I adjusted the seat, feeling the electric motor hum beneath me, and experimented with the radio, switching through stations until I found some calming music.

Despite my attempts to distract myself, my thoughts kept drifting back to Avery. Her determination and strength were evident, but I could see the tension in her shoulders, the slight clenching of her jaw. She was feeling the weight of this mission just as much as I was.

I wanted to say something reassuring; to let her know I trusted her completely, but the words seemed inadequate. Instead, I reached over and squeezed her hand briefly, hoping the gesture would convey what I couldn't put into words.

She glanced at me, a small, grateful smile playing on her lips. "Thanks," she said softly.

As we neared our destination, the tension in the car grew palpable. The landscape around us became more familiar, and the reality of what we were about to do settled heavily in my chest. We had a plan, and I had faith in Avery, but the risks were immense.

"Remember," Avery said, breaking the silence, "We stick to the plan. I'll keep Charles distracted, and you find whatever you can in the basement."

I nodded, trying to push aside my doubts. Richard's thoughts mixed with my own. How could I even bring up his concerns without sounding like a jealous fool? The emotions he harbored were strong and confusing.

"What's on your mind, Nicholas?" Avery asked, breaking through my tangled thoughts. I gulped, not sure how to respond.

"I do not wish to make this car ride any more uncomfortable," I started to explain, but her eyes kept glancing over at me, her lips a straight line of curiosity and concern.

"Um, okay," she said, her tone inviting me to continue.

"However, I do wonder exactly your game plan to keep Charles busy. I know he had forced my wife to kiss him, and I just did not know your intended means of distraction. Coitus should not be on the table." The words felt heavy and awkward as they left my mouth.

"Oh wow, um, we're going here. Okay. I had no plan of coitus. Weird word for sex, by the way. I was just planning on having dinner and honestly talking about, well, you."

"Oh, right," I said, quickly feeling awkwardness filling the air. *Why did you even open your huge mouth? I* asked myself. This poor woman is going through enough emotional upheaval, and here I am a one-hundred-something-year-old spirit living inside her abusive ex's body, being jealous she is having dinner with a vampire. I could see her eyes glancing back at me a few more times. She sighed.

"Now, to be honest, if it was the only way to give you more time, I am willing to do whatever it takes to complete our mission here."

Our eyes connected for a few extra seconds. Her eyes were sincere, and I could see the determination in them. I did not want to think she would have to resort to such measures, but I was grateful to know she understood the gravity of our mission and was willing to do what it took to complete it. It both pained and comforted me to know that she shared my resolve.

We arrived a street over from Charles's home. Avery dropped me off at the bottom of the street.

"Remember, his house is right up there." she explained, pointing at the back of his property. I had to walk up a bit of a hill. "I will keep him busy. When you are finished and cleared out of his house, use this phone to text me. I will make an excuse to leave. Do you remember how to text?"

"I am a scholar. I remember what you taught me," I said, trying to inject some confidence into my voice. I closed the car door after I got out, the chill of the evening air hitting me. I watched as Avery drove away, her car turning to the left.

I stood there for a moment, the weight of what we were about to do settling on my shoulders. This was not just a mission; it was a test of our resolve, our courage, and our willingness to sacrifice for the greater good. I took a deep breath, steeling myself for the task ahead, and began to make my way up the hill towards Charles's house.

I heard something in the distance and froze. Was it the vampire guard? I couldn't be sure, but I wasn't taking any chances. I darted toward an older part of Charles's house, a section that appeared to have been abandoned and left to decay.

The old structure was falling apart, the once-grand façade now a skeleton of its former glory. I stepped inside, the air thick with dust and the scent of mildew. Cobwebs clung to every corner, and the floorboards creaked under my weight.

As I explored, I discovered various relics from Charles's past. There were old spell books, their pages yellowed and brittle, and a broom resting beside a shelf of potion bottles. Its handle was dark with age, carved with faint runes that pulsed under the light, while the bottles beside it shimmered with traces of forgotten spells. The room felt like a time capsule, a glimpse into a world long forgotten.

I found a desk that looked like one from my time and couldn't resist sitting down. The wood was smooth and polished, worn only in places where hands had often touched. As I opened the drawers, I began to search through the shelves, my fingers brushing against long-forgotten trinkets and artifacts. A sense of nostalgia filled the air, the kind that comes from old objects with untold stories. Something caught my eye—a hollow part of the desk. Intrigued, I pried it open and inside was a stack of old photographs wedged behind a shelf. Curious, I pulled them out and began to sift through them. The first was a black-and-white photo of Charles, unmistakably him, though much younger. He had a different hairstyle in each picture, ranging from a clean-cut look to a more rugged, wild appearance. But what struck me was how little he had changed over the years. His face, his eyes-everything was the same. It hit me not as a revelation, but as a reminder of what he truly was—unchanged by time, unburdened by death

As I continued to go through the photos, I saw different women standing beside him in each one. They all had an ethereal quality, beautiful in a timeless sort of way. But what really caught my attention was the subtle similarities they all shared with Emily. The shape of their faces, a certain softness in their eyes, the way they held themselves—it was uncanny. I felt a chill run down my spine. Were these women connected to Emily somehow? Did Charles seek them out because of these resemblances?

A darker thought crossed my mind. Were these women still alive, or had Charles drained them of their blood, leaving them as lifeless husks? The idea of him feeding on them, using them to sustain his eternal life, made my stomach turn. I couldn't help but wonder if he had any real feelings for them or if they were just prey to him, their beauty a mere façade for his true intentions.

"Nicholas…" a faint whisper called to me. It was her voice. Emily's. It drifted through the room like smoke, so soft I almost thought I imagined it. The sound carried a plea, as if calling from somewhere far beyond this world. I stood, turning in a slow circle, scanning the shelves and shadows for any hints. Nothing.

The whisper came again, fainter this time, drawn away by some unseen current. My chest tightened. Something was calling me.

I heard the front door open. My heart raced. Could it be her?

"Hide…" the whisper warned and a wave of panic surged through me. I dropped to the ground, hiding behind the desk. The photographs scattered around me, and I held my breath, praying that whoever it was wouldn't come into this room. A shadow passed across the doorway. Then a voice, low and hungry, slithered through the air.

"I smell you, human. Although, you do have a special smell. One I remember from last week," he hissed.

I pressed myself against the cold floor, my breaths shallow and quiet. The vampire's footsteps were heavy, deliberate, each one echoing through the house like a death knell. I was cornered.

I could hear him moving closer, the scent of old blood and decay growing stronger. I swallowed hard, fighting the urge to gag. He was toying with me, savoring the fear that hung in the air. I had to move, but where? The closet. I scrambled on all fours, slipping into the narrow armoire and pulling its heavy doors shut behind me. The scent of cedar and dust filled my nose. My trembling fingers brushed against the carved wood at my back, tracing uneven edges where the panel didn't quite fit.

The vampire's laughter echoed through the room, low and taunting. "You think you can hide from me? I can hear your heartbeat, feel your fear."

I turned the small latch on the inside of the armoire, sealing the doors. My palms pressed against the back panel again, following a faint seam running along the center. The wood there felt thinner, softer—old. I pushed harder. With a faint creak, the panel shifted and swung inward, revealing a narrow passage carved between the house's walls.

I squeezed through, the rough plaster scraping my arms, and pulled the panel closed behind me. My breaths came fast and shallow in the darkness. Only a thin line of light leaked through the crack where the panel met the wall. My hand slipped into my pocket, pulling out the crumpled piece of paper and the marker.

The marker felt slippery in my sweaty hand as I drew the symbol. Each line had to be perfect; one mistake and it would be useless. My mind raced back to Violet, her calm, steady voice as she taught me how to draw the symbol.

"You'll be okay," she had said, her eyes holding a certainty I wished I shared.

I finished the last stroke just as the closet door crashed open. The vampire's hiss was filled with rage and hunger. He clawed at the barrier, but the symbol held. For now.

"Clever, human. This will only keep you safe for a few minutes. I will find you! I will make sure your death is slow and painful."

I leaned against the wall, my heart pounding. "I'm already in hell. There is nothing more you could do to me."

"We shall see about that," he hissed as he left the closet, his footsteps fading away. I pulled out the phone that Avery gave me. I needed to let her know I needed more time. The glass screen was cracked, and the phone would not turn on.

"Oh no. Did I break this squeezing through the hole in the wall?" I asked myself out loud. I felt so stupid. The darkness pressed in on me, and I knew I had to keep moving. I took a deep breath, steeling myself. I needed to get inside the house to find the amulet and Avery!

Chapter 17

Avery

I pulled my car into his long driveway. It was in the middle of the woods. Talk about some privacy. I couldn't shake off the unease that crept up my spine as I approached his secluded fortress.

My phone sat on the passenger seat, screen dark. I picked it up, checking for the hundredth time to see if Nicholas had messaged me. Nothing. My stomach twisted with worry. What if he forgot how to text me? What if he needed help and I wasn't there to guide him? I bit my lip, trying to push the thoughts away. Focus, Avery.

Charles's house was bigger than mine. It had three levels that I could see from the outside. It was an off-white color with red shingles around certain parts of the home. It looked like a miniature castle, imposing and eerily perfect for someone like

Charles. The kind of place where secrets hid in every shadow, where danger felt as though it lurked just beyond the next corner. I couldn't believe how accurate my dream was about this place.

I glanced at my phone again, willing it to light up with a message from Nicholas. Still nothing. I sighed, anxiety gnawing at my insides. He had to remember. He had to. I'd gone over it with him so many times, drilled it into his head. But what If he panicked and forgot everything? What if he was in trouble right now, and I was wasting time worrying instead of doing something? *No, there is no way he could've found it already. Stop overthinking Avery.*

I took a deep breath, gripping the steering wheel tighter. No, I had to trust him. Nicholas was smart. He'd figure it out.

I stepped out of the car, the cold air biting at my skin. The trees around me seemed to close in, their branches like skeletal fingers reaching out. I shivered, whether from the chill or the nerves, I wasn't sure.

Charles waved at me from the front door. He walked down the wooden stairs meeting me halfway down the driveway. I forced myself to put on the best fake smile I knew how, but my stomach churned.

"Your house is beautiful. Was this a restoration from the Civil War?" I asked, trying to sound casual despite the tightness in my chest.

"It is. If you love the outside, you are going to never want to leave after seeing the inside." He placed his arm on my shoulder to guide me inside. I took a small breath, trying not to show how disgusted I was. His touch made my skin crawl, but I couldn't let him see that.

He was right that I would love the inside. My mouth opened in genuine awe when I saw all the artifacts from around the world. It was like a mini museum. The ceilings were so high up, making the space feel both grand and oppressive. Everything was a warm reddish-brown color, a stark contrast to the coldness I felt from Charles. It felt like a manly home, filled with history and power.

"This stuff is breathtaking. How long have you been collecting?" I looked over at him. He had his hands behind his back, looking down at the floor, a pensive expression on his face.

"Most girls just look at the monetary value of these things. I don't see price tags. I see experience. I see stories." We slowed down as we entered a room full of pictures. Each one depicted different soldiers in battle. I could feel the weight of history in the air, heavy and suffocating.

"Do you have a favorite item?" I asked, trying to keep my voice steady.

"My favorite item in my collection is this photo over here." We walked over to a huge mural that took up half of the wall. Charles just stared at me, his gaze intense and unnerving. I looked closely at one of the men in the mural. It was Charles. My heart skipped a beat.

"Did you go to a reenactment to get this done?" I asked, my voice betraying my attempt at nonchalance.

"Something like that," he said cryptically. I started to look around at the other photos in the room, trying my best to not show him I knew the truth. *He keeps taunting me about his true self. How long has he been doing this?* I thought. The closer I looked, the more I realized they all had Charles in the picture, spanning centuries.

"This is amazing. How did you get these photos digitally done?" I asked, squinting closer.

"It's not."

"Then how?" I asked, genuinely intrigued and increasingly uneasy.

"Magic." He smiled, a smile that didn't reach his eyes. I returned a half-smile, trying to mask my panic. I needed to get us out of this room. I did not want him to know something was off. A whiff of something delicious tantalized my nose, offering a brief distraction.

"What is that aroma?" I asked, following the scent into a different room. Intrigued and grateful for a reason to move away from the haunting photos, we ended up in the dining room. It had huge golden chairs surrounding a long wooden table, the grain of the wood clearly from an older tree, polished to a high shine. White candles were already lit, creating a soft, flickering light. There were two table settings, one at the head of the table, and the other was on the right side. Charles pulled out the chair and gestured for me to sit. I smiled, trying to seem relaxed.

"Thank you," I said, my voice steady despite my nerves.

"You are most welcome. Now, to answer your question. I had the chef make us a three-course meal. The first will be the Caesar salad," Charles explained. He leaned closer to me, speaking lower. "It is the chef's favorite."

"Huge mansion and a chef. How do you afford all of this on our salary?" I asked, my eyebrow raised.

Charles's lips rose into a smirk. "I inherited my money. I only work at the paper for pleasure."

I smiled as two waiters brought out the salad. They had a large selection of different dressings, placing them in front of me.

"Would you like a dressing?" I asked. He shook his head.

"I am afraid I am allergic to garlic. Although the chef tries his best not to include it in any of the ingredients, the dressing he does not make."

I held in a laugh, barely. The absurdity of it all almost made me forget the danger I was in. Almost.

"Where are my manners? I forgot to offer you some red wine. Would you care to join me for a drink?" he asked.

"Sure." I replied, trying to keep my voice steady. As he bowed his head slightly, a gesture that seemed out of place for this century, it made me think of Nicholas. I hoped he was able to get in the house. The thought of him navigating through the shadows gave me a brief, flickering hope. I slowly took my cell from my pocket. No new messages. This was going to be harder than I thought.

Charles poured the wine with a practiced elegance, the deep red liquid swirling into the glass like blood. I couldn't help but feel a shiver of apprehension. Every detail, every move he made seemed designed to remind me of what he was. What he could do. Does he already know I know?

I took a sip, the wine warm and rich on my tongue, but my mind was elsewhere. I had to stay focused. I had to keep my composure. My thoughts raced, darting between the artifacts that filled the room and the conversation we just had. He was taunting me, testing me, and I had to play along.

"So," I said, trying to keep my voice light, "What's the main course?"

He smiled, his eyes glinting with a predatory gleam. "Ah, that would be a surprise. Patience."

I forced another smile, my fingers tightening around the stem of the wine glass. I couldn't let him see through my façade. Not yet. I needed more time to figure out his game. More time for Nicholas to make his move. My heart pounded in my chest, but I took a deep breath and steadied myself.

We made small talk as we ate the salad, Charles watching me with an intensity that made my skin crawl. I could feel the weight of his gaze, the unspoken threat that lingered beneath his charming exterior. Each bite was a struggle, my mind racing with thoughts of escape, of survival.

As the waiters cleared our plates and brought out the next course, I glanced at my phone again, hoping for some sign from Nicholas. Still nothing. I bit back a curse, forcing myself to remain calm. Charles couldn't know how close we were to the truth. He couldn't know that his games were wearing thin.

I took another sip of wine, bracing myself for whatever came next. This was a dangerous dance, and one misstep could be my last. But I had to keep going. I had to find a way to turn the tables. And I had to trust that Nicholas would come through.

"So, did you go back to the museum at all?" Charles asked. I shook my head, feeling a strange mix of nervousness and curiosity.

"Thank you. No. I wanted to, but I just suddenly got very overwhelmed with the information," I stated, taking a small sip of wine. It had such a strong taste, almost metallic, lingering on my tongue. "I did want to apologize for the way I've been acting."

"Yes, what did happen? I was confused about what I had said to make you fear me." Charles's gaze softened, his concern seeming genuine, but there was an underlying intensity that made me uneasy.

"I moved here into my deceased aunt's house because I was running away from my ex," I began, my voice trembling slightly as I recalled the painful memories.

"Oh my," Charles responded, leaning forward slightly, his eyes locked onto mine.

"Yes. He had beaten me severely. He was in jail. The police told me I should look for somewhere else to live," I said, taking a bigger gulp of wine, the taste now mingling with the bitterness of my memories. "When you grabbed my face that day, I had a flashback of him doing that to me. And then you were being overbearing with this Nicholas Blackstone article. I had a moment."

We sat there in silence for a few moments, the weight of my confession hanging in the air. Charles's expression was inscrutable, his eyes thoughtful, but I couldn't shake the feeling that there was something he wasn't telling me.

A loud crashing noise made us both jump. I looked over at Charles. His eyes were staring straight ahead, but his head was slightly turned toward the direction of the noise. *Shit, was that the basement? Is Nicholas okay?* I wondered, anxiety prickling at the edges of my mind. Charles took his cloth napkin and wiped his face with an eerie calmness. Then he smiled at me, a smile that didn't reach his eyes.

"Please excuse me. I must see what the new maid is getting into." He stood up and slightly bowed to me, his manners contrasting sharply with the growing sense of dread in my chest. Maybe he was right. Maybe it was just the maid or one of his other servants. He must have a lot of money to have all of this help.

I looked down at my phone, hoping to see the number one above the text message speech bubble. There were none, though. I blinked, trying to see the screen a little clearer, but the images started to blur. Panic set in as I placed my hand on my head, feeling the room spin around me. The wine glass slipped from my fingers, shattering on the floor. I tried to stand up, but my legs gave way, and my body collided with the cold, hard floor.

One of the butlers walked in and pulled me by my arm. His grip was firm, almost mechanical, and I tried to resist, but my strength was fading fast.

"Help me," I softly whispered, my voice barely audible as darkness closed in around me. The last thing I saw was the butler's impassive face, his eyes void of any compassion. Everything went dark.

Chapter 18

Nicholas

The tunnel was dark and narrow, the air damp and musty. I moved cautiously, my hand trailing along the rough stone walls. Each step echoed in the confined space, a constant reminder of how alone I was. My heart pounded in my chest, each beat echoing in my ears as I wondered what lay at the end of this path.

After what felt like an eternity, my fingers brushed against something cold and metallic—a doorknob. I turned it, but the door wouldn't budge. Frustration bubbled up inside me. I took a few steps back, steeling myself. There was no other way. I had to force it open.

I ran at the door with all my strength, slamming my shoulder into it. The wood cracked and gave way with a loud crash, and I stumbled forward, falling into a dimly lit basement. Pain shot through my shoulder, but I ignored it, quickly getting to my feet. The basement was small, cluttered with old furniture and boxes. There was only one door to get in and out.

For a moment, the silence was broken by a faint whisper. *"Nicholas…"*

It was her again—Emily. The sound was weaker now, echoing through the stone walls as though carried from another realm. *"Hurry,"* the voice urged, fading to nothing.

I froze, unsure if it was in my head or something beyond this world guiding me. Either way, I listened. I had to keep moving.

I approached the door quietly, pressing my ear against it. Voices echoed from somewhere above—too many to be Charles alone. I turned the knob and eased the door open, slipping into the hallway beyond. The voices were louder now, but distant. I moved quickly, keeping to the shadows.

A door to my left caught my eye. I slipped inside, closing it quietly behind me. The room was a study, lavishly decorated with dark wood paneling and shelves filled with ancient books and artifacts. The scent of leather and old paper filled the air. I took a moment to catch my breath, the adrenaline still coursing through my veins.

Just as I turned to leave, footsteps approached the study. My heart raced. There was no time. I darted behind a large, heavy curtain just as the door creaked opened.

Several sets of footsteps entered, slow and deliberate, the sound of boots tapping against the hardwood floor. I swallowed hard, bile rising in my throat. The scent of old blood drifted through the air, thick and metallic.

Charles's voice filled the room, commanding and impatient. "Is everything in order here?"

"Yes, sir. Nothing seems out of place," a man replied.

"Good. Keep it that way," Charles said, his tone dripping with arrogance.

I held my breath, the heavy fabric brushing against my face. Then came a pause. The faint scrape of boots against wood.

Charles inhaled sharply, the sound low and feral. I went still as stone. He was *smelling* the air.

For a long, dreadful moment, he didn't move. Then a faint scowl colored his words. "Something's off..."

My pulse thundered. Had he caught my scent?

But then he exhaled through his nose, almost dismissively. "Probably the stench of the tunnel. Have it scrubbed."

"Yes, sir," the servant said quickly.

Charles and the servant began to leave, their footsteps echoing toward the hall. I waited, every muscle in my body tight as a bowstring. The moment the door clicked shut, I let out a slow breath.

Then I felt it—like a hum in the air. A pulse. Subtle at first, then stronger. The same sensation I'd felt before, when I'd heard Emily's voice.

"Nicholas..."

Her whisper brushed against my ear, softer than a sigh.

My eyes drifted toward the desk. Something about it felt... alive. I crouched, running my fingers along the edge of the drawer until I saw faint engravings burned into the wood—symbols I recognized instantly.

The markings matched those etched into the blade Emily had given me before I died—the dragon knife. My chest tightened as I drew it from my belt, the metal catching what little light filtered through the curtains. The dragon's sapphire eyes gleamed to life, glowing faintly.

Guided by instinct, I pressed the knife's tail into a narrow slit along the side of the desk. A soft *click* echoed through the silence, followed by a deeper *pop*. A hidden panel in the desktop sprang open, revealing a small velvet-lined compartment.

Inside lay the amulet.

It glowed faintly, as though breathing, its light pulsing in rhythm with my own heartbeat. The instant my fingers brushed it, a rush of cold air swept through the room. For a heartbeat, I swore I heard Emily's voice again—distant, sorrowful.

"Find me."

The light dimmed. The air went still. I pocketed the amulet, my pulse thundering in my ears.

Avery

An achy, sharp pain overtook the top of my skull. Panic surged through me as I reached to grab my head, but something held my arms still. I tugged harder. My mind raced, trying to make sense of what was going on. A cold sweat broke out on my forehead as my heart rate quickened. Light from what I assumed was a lamp shone brightly as I slowly forced open my eyes, and the glare forced me to squint.

"Ugh," I moaned in agony. The room spun as I struggled to focus. Where was I? Fear gnawed at my mind as I pulled on my arms again, and I heard a clanking noise that startled me. I fluttered my eyes a few times, trying to adjust to the surroundings—dread hit my gut. How did I end up bound?

"Who's there?" I asked in a shaky voice as footsteps echoed ominously against the walls.

"Ah, good! You're up. You've been a naughty girl, haven't you?" A familiar voice laughed, sending shivers down my spine. The person stepped closer, and I blinked a few times, my heart racing. It was Charles.

"What are you talking about? Why am I tied up? Is this some odd newspaper initiation prank?" I asked, attempting to mask my rising panic. Did he figure out what we were doing? My mind raced through the possibilities.

As he approached, the weight of his presence pressed down on me. I realized then that I was tied to a sturdy wooden chair—my wrists bound to the armrests, my ankles to the legs. Charles moved around me slowly, like a predator circling its prey. Then, with a sudden yank, he dragged my chair forward across the floor, closer to him. The screech of wood against tile pierced the silence, and my pulse spiked.

He crouched down in front of me, his movements deliberate and controlled, his face now inches from mine.

"Better," he murmured, his gaze locking onto mine.

I tried to pull away, but the restraints held firm. It felt like he held my face, though his hands weren't touching me. I could see them in my peripheral vision, casually on his knees. A cold sweat trickled down my neck. His eyes bore into mine, an unsettling mixture of amusement and malice.

"Charles, this isn't funny. Please release me!" I begged. Why did he have me restrained? The air felt thicker with each passing second. I yanked on the rope, desperate to break free. Heat overtook my wrists.

"What do you want from me?" I demanded, trying to keep my voice steady.

"Ah, that sneaky man," he scoffed, his voice dripping with contempt. I kept telling myself to pull away, but my body betrayed me. What man was he talking about? Why was he staring at me like this? Slight specks of gold illuminated his pupils, casting an eerie glow. I tried to move my face, but my brain seemed paralyzed, locked in place by some unseen force. Charles continued to look into my eyes, his gaze like a vice grip. When he finally sat back on his heels and shook his head, I could breathe again, my body trembling with relief.

"What did you do to me?" I demanded, my voice quivering with anger. Charles stood, his cold hand brushing my cheek with a chilling tenderness.

"We could make such a strong power couple. Why would you want to destroy me?"

"What are you talking about?" I asked, my head spinning with confusion and fear.

"You can stop pretending, little witch," he said, a cruel smile playing on his lips. I gasped, my heart pounding. "Yes, your friends are right about me. I am the eldest of vampires. Yes, I have daddy and mommy issues."

He straightened to his full height, then leaned forward again, resting one hand on the arm of my chair and the other on the backrest—caging me in.

"I don't want to kill you," he whispered, his tone darkly reverent. "I want you to be my bride. I've felt the power you have." He leaned closer, his breath cold against my skin, his lips curling back to reveal sharp canines that gleamed in the dim light. "With your power and my ability to make people do anything I want, we would be unstoppable. I could make you the first vamp witch."

"So, what? Would you bite me or something?"

"No, I already poisoned you. All I'd have to do is snap your neck," he said, his tongue swiping over his canine, a predatory glint in his eyes.

"Poisoned me with what?" I snapped, my wrists straining against the ropes. If I could get him to keep talking, maybe Nicholas would show up with the amulet, or I could get my hands free. Either one would work.

"My blood, of course. That's one thing the movies got right," Charles laughed, the sound cold and mirthless. "I just dropped some in your wine. It tasted divine, didn't it? It's the only way to weaken witches."

"So, you already knew I was a witch?"

"Not one hundred percent. I had an inkling you could be because of your aunt. I figured if you were a witch, it would weaken you. If you were a normal human, well, the power of my blood would enflame your passion for me. Win-win."

I didn't know how to take all this information. I continued moving my fingertips to the rope, my heart racing with every second.

"Eww, you know you're like my great-great-great-great-whatever-grandfather, right?" I said, trying to mask my fear with disgust.

"We wouldn't be the first sexual relatives." Charles shrugged nonchalantly. I stared at him, my skin crawling. "I'll give you a little while to think about this."

Charles started to walk towards the door. My mind raced, desperate to come up with another distraction. "So, if I agree to this, will you untie me?"

"Oh, my dear, you're adorable! I wouldn't untie you. I'd kill you, and then when you wake up, you'll want to feed. I won't let you just go kill anyone. We have a reputation to uphold in this town. I'd have only the best blood available to you."

He walked closer, his sharp fingernail trailing down my arm, sending shivers down my spine. He smiled at me, a predator enjoying his prey.

"What do you mean 'the best blood available to you?'" I asked, trying to keep his attention. My fingertip finally slid slightly into the knot. Charles chuckled, amused by my attempt.

"After all these years, you don't think we just drink any blood, do you?" Charles stared at me, his gaze piercing. "We made a pact with Emily Blackstone years ago that we'd only take blood from willing out-of-towners."

"The animal attacks, that was you?" I asked. Charles nodded.

"Guilty as charged. We had some newborn vamps not fully listening to the rules. But that's why it's so important the blood you drink when you first turn. It decides your control."

Charles sat back down, his movements restless. I worried he'd catch me trying to untie myself.

"So, is there a certain out-of-towner I would drink?"

"Well, I could get you an out-of-towner. Or I could give you more of my blood. When you're fully willing to drink my blood, not just have it hidden in your cup, you'll be sired to me."

"Sired?" I asked. Charles placed his forehead against mine, his breath hot and unnervingly intimate.

"Yes, my dear. Your whole being will be devoted to me. Every thought, every need, and every urge will be to please me."

"But you can make anyone anywhere do what you want."

"Except you," his voice deepened with a chill, his eyes narrowing. "I want and need control over the one witch who has the power to kill me."

The need to get these restraints off became urgent, my fingers sweating and slipping off the rope. Smelling my neck, his new favorite thing, he drew closer. I closed my eyes tightly, fighting the panic rising within me.

A clanking noise by the door startled us. Charles growled, his forehead still pressed against mine.

"I guess that's Nicholas out there, huh?" Charles growled. His eyes flashed gold again, the intensity almost unbearable. He stood up, pacing back and forth, his fingers rubbing his bare chin. One of the butlers entered the room. Charles looked up at him, and the butler bowed, his eyes averted.

"Did you find him?" The butler hesitated, then shook his head. Charles sighed, exasperated. "Well, if you want something done, you should just do it yourself." Charles shrugged at me and exited the room in a blur. My chest heaved with rapid breaths as I squirmed in the chair.

"Come on, you freaking rope!" I muttered; my eyes darted to the door as more clanking occurred. Sweat dripped down my face, and I inhaled deeply, trying to refocus.

"Okay, Avery. What did Violet teach you? Just remember." I closed my eyes, searching my mind for any spell or protection. "Any day now."

My mind was blank, panic rising as I realized I needed to escape now. Richard's hateful words echoed in my mind, every insult fueling my desperation.

"You are worthless. Your mother should have swallowed you; instead, you are here tormenting me. That's why she died. To escape you."

My chest rose quicker with each horrid thing he said. I felt a suffocating weight in my chest, the pressure making it hard to breathe.

"I can't do this. I'm going to die here," I thought, my resolve weakening. My fingers slipped from the rope again, slick with sweat. The sensation of the coarse fibers biting into my skin sent jolts of pain through my arms, each failed attempt chipping away at my confidence.

"I'm not strong enough. I never was." Tears of frustration stung my eyes, blurring my vision. I was so close, yet so far from freedom. The knot felt like it was mocking me, refusing to budge no matter how hard I pulled.

In a desperate attempt to calm myself, I thought about Nicholas. Somewhere in this house, he believed in me. Violet taught me all these things because she believed I could do it. But what if they were wrong? What if I wasn't the hero they thought I was?

Hoping to stay focused, I hummed to myself, trying to drown out the rising panic. "Okay, Avery, you got this. You're freaking Avery Jones. You're the only witch in the bloodline strong enough to stop him. Believe in yourself."

My voice cracked, and the doubt crept back in. "I can't even free myself. How am I supposed to defeat him?" I closed my eyes, held my breath, and yanked my hands one last time. The rope didn't budge.

"Come on!" I yelled in frustration, the sound echoing in the empty room. Failure took over my mind, and I slumped in the chair, defeated. How could I defeat the eldest vampire if I couldn't free myself? What was I thinking? I could never be the hero in any story.

A jiggling noise came from the direction of the door. Left, then right, the door handle moved. My heart pounded in my chest. I did not want to be a witch vamp hybrid. Nicholas peeped his head into the door. I never thought I would be this excited to see my ex's face.

"Nicholas!" I shouted. He looked over at me, then his eyes scanned the room.

"Miss Avery. I'm so glad I found you," he said softly. "I was worried he did something to you."

He ran to me and started to tug on the rope. I could feel it starting to loosen slightly.

"What kind of knot is this?" Nicholas said, annoyed.

"The kind you can't untie," a voice boomed from the doorway.

Nicholas flew across the room into the wall beside me.

Charles leaned against the door frame, arms crossed, a faint smirk tugged at his lips.

"Well, well," he drawled. "We meet again."

Nicholas straightened, fury in his eyes. "Charles."

Chapter 19

Nicholas

"Ah, Nicholas, this must be the new body you took from Avery's ex. At least this one isn't as weak and useless as the old one. I thought I got rid of you all those years ago. Obviously, you're as hard to kill as a roach," Charles sneered, his voice dripping with malice.

"The only annoying pest here is you. How could you betray me? How could you kill my Emily?" I retorted, my voice trembling with a mix of rage and sorrow.

"Your Emily? She didn't even feel comfortable telling you who she was! What kind of marriage is that?" Charles questioned, a mocking smile playing on his lips.

"I do not know how I would have reacted, but she chose to never give me that chance. I regret that she felt the need to hide who she was," I said, my gaze dropping to the floor.

"Don't let him mess with your head, Nicholas!" Avery yelled from across the room. Charles's eyes flickered toward her, his eyebrows furrowing.

"Little witch, little witch. What am I going to do with you?" Charles asked, tilting his head to the side. "I have twenty-four hours to read your mind. To make you do my bidding."

"Then kill me already. Make me do everything you want," Avery yelled sarcastically.

Charles's eyes glinted with malicious amusement as he approached Avery. He grabbed her chin roughly, forcing her to look into his eyes. "No more talking," he commanded, his voice low and hypnotic. Avery's eyes glazed over, her lips pressing together as she struggled against the compulsion but was unable to speak another word.

I stood in front of Avery, my protective instinct kicking in. "You will not hurt Miss Avery," I said, using a stronger tone. Charles raised one eyebrow, a half-smile overtaking his face.

"And what can you do?" Charles asked, circling around us, getting closer. "You couldn't save your Emily back then. What makes you think anything has changed?"

"I know who you truly are now. This is what changed," I said.

Before I could react, Charles lifted his hand, and with a flick of his wrist, I was thrown across the room again by an invisible force. I crashed into the wall with a grunt, the impact knocking the wind out of me. Charles laughed darkly, his eyes gleaming with satisfaction.

I screamed as I lunged my body into Charles. We both fell to the ground. The amulet popped out of my pocket and fell inches from Avery's feet where she sat, still tied up.

"I have so many questions. I thought vampires didn't age," I said, my voice strained as I fought to catch my breath.

"We don't age. At least I didn't until your wife tried to turn me human. I seem to age very slowly, and at one hundred years, I went back to my youthful self. I'll find out in about fifty more years if I'll go back again," Charles scoffed, his voice tinged with arrogance.

"Is that why you killed Emily?" I yelled, tears streaming down my face as my breathing grew heavy and labored.

"Calm down, Nicky boy. You don't want to have a stroke in that new body of yours, do you?" Charles taunted, walking to the other side of the room. Avery's whimpers filled the air, tears streaming down her face. Charles pulled out a cigarette from his shirt pocket, lighting it without ever taking his eyes off me. He approached Avery, touching her face with a sickening familiarity. He licked and kissed her neck, causing her to squeeze her eyes shut in terror. My body tensed with rage.

"Nooooo!" I screamed. "Don't you hurt her or I swear I will kill you."

"There is my Nicky boy, willing to do whatever it takes to protect the ones he loves," Charles laughed. "Tell me, how does it feel to know you failed to save Emily?"

Before I could react, Charles closed the distance between us and punched me in the stomach. Pain exploded through my body as I crumpled to the ground.

"You're a monster," I cried, grasping for breath.

"So, you don't like seeing Avery hurt, huh?" Charles's eyes glowed red as he puffed on his cigarette. He took a knife and slowly traced it up Avery's thigh. Her chest heaved with fear as she cried.

"What do you want? Don't hurt her!" I pleaded, desperation creeping into my voice.

"What do I want? I want to watch you suffer," Charles said, his voice cold and devoid of any humanity.

As he continued to taunt and torment us, I knew I had to find a way to save Avery and end this nightmare once and for all. Summoning every ounce of strength and determination, I prepared myself for the fight of my life. Charles turned his back towards me. Avery cried out more as Charles cut her shirt off her. Every muscle in my body contracted, steaming in anger. I screamed as I charged towards Charles.

I knocked him off his feet. I watched as his knife slid across the floor, away from Avery. I knew I had seconds to grab the knife, the amulet, and free Avery. I slid across the ground, the knife easily within reach.

Charles's shoulder rammed into my body like a wrecking ball. My body catapulted across the room. I picked my head up, shaking it, my body feeling as if every bone was crushed. I looked up to see I was now in front of Avery! For a split second, hope was attainable.

I sat up and glanced at Avery and then the amulet. Which should I go for first? The amulet was useless if Avery's hands were tied.

"Everything is going to be okay," I said as I slipped the knife between the knotted coils of rope, separating its fibers with the blade. I barely had the blade halfway through when my whole body was thrown across the floor again.

"Ha, you almost had me. Alas, I am the eldest vampire in the world, and it will take a lot more than that to kill me." Charles's eyes glowed a bright red with each step he took. He raised his hands, throwing me to the other wall.

I tried catching my breath, the impact knocking the wind out of me again. I looked over at Avery. The knife fell to the ground. "Is that the best you got?" I winced in pain, trying to sit back up. "The Charles I remembered had a lot more vengeance. Perhaps you have gotten soft in your old age."

"Soft. I remember that is what they said about you when you first joined the army." Charles grabbed me by the throat, raising me off the ground. My hands reached into my pocket, my fingertips grazing the small vial of garlic dust Violet had given me. Charles's smile widened with each second I was deprived of air.

I twisted the vial open, flinging the powder into his face. He screamed, stumbling backward, clutching his burning eyes. I collapsed to the floor, gasping for air, my vision tunneling.

The door to the study burst open, the sound of splintering wood echoing through the mansion. A pulse of energy rippled through the room, scattering the shadows.

Violet stepped through first, her hands glowing with light.

"How—" I coughed, dragging myself up.

"We've been tracking you since the moment your signal rune went dark," she said quickly, raising her hand toward Avery. The ropes disintegrated into ash as magic pulsed from her fingertips.

Behind her, Marcus and Lucien fought through the doorway—Marcus's claws tearing through two vampire guards who tried to follow. "They had half the damn coven's blood charm on the entrance," Marcus growled, wiping his mouth. "Took us long enough to break it."

Elara appeared next, chanting under her breath as a shimmering barrier flared across the threshold. "That'll keep his soldiers out for a few minutes."

Charles roared, smoke curling from his face as the garlic ate into his skin. "You meddling pests!"

Charles's attention flickered momentarily to the new arrivals. Violet glanced at him, her expression fierce.

I looked over at Avery, trying to pull in as much air as I could. She rushed to retrieve the amulet. Charles stopped coughing. His eyes observed that I was no longer watching him. He followed my eyeline to see Avery was out of her rope.

Before he could react, Marcus lunged at him, transforming mid-air into his werewolf form. His claws slashed at Charles, driving him back. Lucien, moving with inhuman speed, was at Marcus's side, his vampire fangs bared. The two supernatural beings attacked in unison, forcing Charles into a defensive stance.

Elara's eyes glowed with a soft, ethereal light as she chanted under her breath, casting protective spells around us. Violet joined in, her hands weaving intricate patterns in the air, adding her own magical strength to the fight.

I scrambled to my feet, still catching my breath. "Avery, the amulet!" I shouted, my voice hoarse.

Charles snarled, his strength formidable even against the combined forces of Marcus and Lucien. He broke free of their grasp, his eyes blazing with fury. "You think you can defeat me?" he roared. "I am eternal!"

Marcus growled, his powerful form towering over Charles. "You are not invincible, Vampire. We will end you."

Violet's magic shimmered in the air, forming a protective barrier around Avery. Elara's spells bolstered Marcus and Lucien, giving them the edge they needed to keep Charles at bay.

Avery clutched the amulet tightly, her eyes meeting mine across the chaos. I nodded at her, a silent message of encouragement. The runes along the amulet began to glow, but the light flickered like a heartbeat.

Charles's gaze shifted, sharp and predatory, landing on Avery. "Ah," he hissed. "There it is."

Charles took a step towards Avery, but Marcus and Lucien lunged onto him, driving Charles toward the wall.

"Keep him pinned!" Violet shouted.

The amulet flared brighter, responding to Avery's spell. Her lips moved quickly, reciting the incantation Violet had drilled into her. The air grew heavy, vibrating with power.

But Charles's laughter cut through the chaos. "You think that trinket can kill me?" His body twisted, strength surging again as he shoved Marcus aside. He crawled through Lucien's grip, his eyes glowing with renewed fury. "You've never faced real power, little witch."

The amulet's light flickered violently. Avery staggered, her knees hitting the floor as she tried to hold her focus. "Violet!" she gasped. "I–I can't contain it!"

Violet turned toward her; eyes wide. "Don't stop! He's fighting it–he's trying to drain the spell."

Charles advanced, each step heavy with power, his veins darkening as he resisted the pull of the amulet's magic. "You can't stop me, girl," he hissed. "You'll burn before I do."

Avery screamed as a burst of light flared from the amulet, forcing his back a few feet–but the glow around her dimmed.

I stepped forward instinctively. "She can't hold it! It's going to kill her!"

"Don't you dare!" Violet snapped, grabbing my arm. "That magic will pull both yours and Richard's soul and drag you to hell. It's pure life energy."

Charles stumbled, then steadied, still coming. "It's over, witch."

The room went silent and in slow motion as I watched Avery. Sweat fell down her face, and I no longer could breathe.

We need to save her, Richard. I said in my mind. Doing the only thing my mind could think of. *We need to let go of this body.*

It will kill us! Richard's voice said weakly. *I'm not ready to die.*

You're going to die either way, and you know it. And I am on borrowed time. I said, watching as Marcus and Lucien tried knocking Charles to the ground. Charles moved his body swiftly, and bit into Marcus's neck, blood now dripping out. *She deserves better than anything we could give her. No matter how much we love her.*

Richard was quiet in my mind for a few seconds. *Save her.* He finally said, and I didn't hesitate. I ran towards Charles, closing my eyes when I was a few steps away. Richard's body tingled as my soul left and entered Charles.

"Nicholas, no!" Avery yelled as I opened my eyes in Charles's body. I inhaled a few deep breaths as I forced control from

Charles, whose hands were inches from Avery's neck. I stared into her gorgeous eyes, and my lips rose upwards.

What the hell are you doing, Nicholas? Charles hissed in my head.

Saving the world the only way I know how. I said, struggling to beat him inside our mind. He was more challenging that Richard was since he had no alcohol in his system.

Don't be stupid. Yes, you will kill me, but you will go to hell. Charles said with a grunt. I pushed back, trying to stay in control of his body.

How appropriate. I've got a seat reserved right next to yours. I said back with more power. I glanced at Avery and saw the stake poking out from under her jacket. I took a step towards her, placing my forehead on hers. My body tingled as I was swept away in her blue eyes. I don't know what took over me. Was it residuals from Richard's body? Was it the lust from Charles's body? Or could it really be from me?

The truth hit me. It wasn't Richard's habit or his hunger that made my chest ache; it was the small things–the way Avery chewed the corner of her lip when she was thinking, the half-smile she gave when she tried to hide how proud she was, and the small moan she does with her first sip of coffee.

Those tiny, private things lived in my bones. My throat tightened. My hands trembled to reach for her because I wanted her safe for reasons that belonged only to me. Not pity or borrowed grief. Not Richard's memories. Me.

I closed my eyes and let that realization land. It didn't make the fear any smaller, but it made everything else sharper.

"Finish him, Avery. Save us all." I said, forcing out in pain as I let the guard down Charles had around his body.

Avery's blue eyes widened as she realized what I had done. A tear left her eye while she stood up, her lips moving again as she said her incantation.

I could feel Charles's body weakening with every word that came from her mouth. His canine teeth shrunk back into his gums. The animal instincts wavered. Flashes of Charles's life as a vampire sped past my eyes. Countless of woman being turned, trying to relive his time with Emily, but none of them could compare. My heart ached slightly as I could feel the heartache and want of Emily in his body. There was another part of his memory that I couldn't see, something deep in a dark box.

As the memories slowed down to the start of his vampirism, I could see the longing of just wanting to be accepted by his father and mother. Suddenly, his humanity turned on as Avery's words stopped. A pulse of power flew through us, and no heavy darkness clouded our mind.

It's over, Charles. Now, you're human. I said, feeling my soul weakening slightly from using so much power to fight him.

Avery ran over to me and hugged me. "We did it Nicholas!" She placed her hand on my chest, and tingles took over my body. Her blue eyes stared into mine with a hesitant look, trying to get passed the latest body.

"I know, it's weird." I said, letting her know I understand her mindset. Her lips arched up, and God would I do anything to keep that smile on her face.

The adrenaline from the fight still coursed through me, and I had the need to taste her lips one time before I left this world.

I caressed her cheeks, and to my surprise, she didn't shy away. Our eyes stayed connected as we leaned closer.

No! I will kill her! Charles screamed in my mind just as Avery's lips grazed mine. I pushed her back, knocking her down. I grabbed my head, fighting the urge to want to hit her. Charles, even as a human, had a strong mental presence, and mine was weakening. I could see in my mind what he was thinking about doing to her. He wanted to place his hands around her neck until it snapped. I would never let that happen.

I realized I had the stake still in my hand. I glanced over at her and smiled before giving her any chance to tell me to stop, I plunged it into Charles's chest.

I felt a stabbing pain before a release of relief took over Charles's body. His soul had left as I fell to my knees. Avery rushed over to me and caught me before I fell backwards. A cold numbness spread from the wound, the edges of my vision blurring as my life force left me. I felt Avery's arms around me, her warmth a stark contrast to the chill overtaking Charles's body.

"Nicholas, no," Avery's voice wavered, tears streaming down her face. I could barely make out her words, but the sorrow in her eyes spoke volumes.

I managed a weak smile, my strength fading fast. "It's alright, Avery," I whispered, each word a struggle. "We stopped him, and you're safe now. That's all that matters."

The room seemed to blur, supernatural beings surrounding us. Violet knelt beside me, her eyes filled with a mix of sorrow and gratitude. She placed a hand on my forehead, a soothing warmth emanating from her touch.

"You both did it. You saved us all," Violet said softly, her voice carrying a sense of reverence.

The others joined in, their expressions reflecting their appreciation. Marcus, Elara, and Lucien all nodded in acknowledgment.

I felt the room tilt, time slowing like syrup, so I pushed the words out gentle and small. "Take care of each other. Don't waste what we made here. Help Avery mend what can be mended and…" I said until a cough forced itself from Charles's lungs. Faces blurred as Charles's body shivered. I swallowed hard. "Bring the supernatural beings together. We are stronger that way."

I swallowed hard before I looked back at Avery, her blue eyes filled with tears. "I don't regret this. We were destined to meet."

Avery's lips arched upwards as she nodded her head, her grip tightening around me as if trying to hold onto my fading essence. My vision darkened, and I felt my consciousness slipping away.

With my last breath, I whispered, "Emily… I'll see you soon."

Everything went black, a serene void enveloping me as I left the world behind, knowing I had done my part.

Chapter 20

Avery- 5 days later

Nicholas haunted me more now than he did when he was a ghost. That night played in my head every time I was alone or closed my eyes. Charles's lips on mine when Nicholas was inside his body should have disgusted me. Charles was the one trying to kill me. But my heart knew it was Nicholas. I could feel his kindness and determination radiating through that body as he looked at me.

I don't regret this. We were destined to meet. Nicholas's last words echoed in my mind. I should have said more to him, but we didn't have the time. He needed to know I didn't regret it either.

The scent of coffee and cinnamon brought me back to the present. The hum of the diner filled the air—murmured conversations, clinking dishes, the low buzz of an old jukebox in the corner.

Violet sat across from me, stirring her coffee absently as she finished reading my article–the one about Nicholas and Emily Blackstone's journals, their love, and their tragedy. Writing it had nearly broken me, but my editor had a few tears drop from her eyes when she read it, which shocked and pleased me.

Violet lowered the newspaper, a tear slipping down her cheek. "This was a beautiful tribute to him. He would've loved it."

I nodded, a small, forced smile graced my lips. "I can't stop replaying that night in my head. Every time I think about what he did, it just... doesn't seem fair."

Violet sighed and reached across the table grabbing my hand. "He made his choice, Avery. He wanted to save you. And would do it again in a heartbeat."

I looked down at my coffee, watching the steam curl upward. I let go of her hand, so I could take a drink of my coffee.

"He shouldn't have had to make that choice at all. If I would've been stronger," I said, my voice cracking as I fought the tears.

We sat in silence for a few minutes, looking out the diner window. Cars passed by, people laughed, and life continued as if nothing had happened.

"I miss him," I said finally, the words small but heavy.

Violet smiled sadly. "We all do."

My eyebrows furrowed as I exhaled shakily. "It just feels wrong sitting here, drinking coffee like everything is normal. I need to do something. I need to at least know if he can't be here with me, he's with Emily."

"Well, he wanted us all to work together and make a better life for all the supernatural beings. It's time we make this town the first safe haven for all beings." Violet said. My eyebrow raised at the thought of that. Getting all the beings to live in harmony would be nice. "Maybe we can start by having a memorial for Nicholas? I'm sure we can find some pictures of just him or him and Emily."

My lips curled up, "A memorial?" I repeated. "A small get together with the others, honoring him. We could remind them what he wanted and start bringing them together. I like it."

Violet's eyes softened. "Then we'll make it happen."

The next night, the old town hall was filled with candlelight and pictures of Nicholas that Lucien borrowed from the museum. Beings from every corner of the supernatural world had come—witches, werewolves, vampires, and elves.

Elara and the elves sang elvish tunes that talked about passing on. Then, Violet spoke first, her voice steady despite the emotion behind it. "Nicholas showed us what strength really means. Sacrifice, compassion, and courage."

I stepped forward, my gaze sweeping the room. "With his last words he wanted us to move forward together. I think the best way to honor him is to try to make a world where vampires and elves can go to school together. He loved teaching more than anything. I want to go to work and see werewolves and witches grocery shopping together. Do you think we can at least try?"

A murmur of agreement rippled through the crowd. For a moment, it felt like peace might be possible. Then the large town hall doors swung open.

A group of vampires, led by one of the guards that were at Charles's house, strode inside.

Lucien stood in front of me. "Adrian, this isn't the time or place."

"Oh Luci," Adrian said with a mocking grin. "I'm just here to watch all of you mourn your fallen hero. And to remind you who the eldest vampire is now. We will *never* bow down or work together with any of you."

He turned to leave, but I stepped in front of Lucien. "Wait, I beg you to reconsider. Nicholas wanted..."

In an instant, Adrian was inches from my face. "Let's get this straight, witch," he hissed. "I don't fucking care what he wanted."

His eyes trailed down my body before he leaned closer, inhaling deeply. When his eyes connected with mine, his pupils were crimson with black veins spidering beneath the surface. "But I'd love to see you begging on your knees."

"Never... happening." I said, my voice shaking but defiant. I barely recognized my own voice. His lips curved into a cruel smile before he vanished, the wind from his exit slamming the doors shut.

"So much for peace." Violet said.

"Maybe," I said, my eyes never leaving the door. "But Nicholas always found a way, and we will too."

The night was eerily quiet as I prepared for bed, the events of the day weighing heavily on my mind. Nicholas's memorial had been emotionally draining, and the confrontation with Adrian left me feeling more unsettled than ever. As I changed into my nightgown and brushed my hair, Adrians's words repeated in my mind and the way he sniffed me, made the hairs on my arm stand up.

I climbed into bed, pulling the covers up to my chin, but sleep refused to come. I tossed and turned, trying to find a comfortable position, but the unease only grew stronger.

Suddenly, a strange humming filled the room, making the hairs on the back of my neck stand on end. I sat up abruptly, my heart pounding. The air in the corner of my room shimmered, warping and twisting as if reality itself was being torn apart. A swirling portal of dark energy appeared, and I froze.

My breath caught when a tall figure stepped through the vortex. For a moment, my heart soared–his silhouette, his stance, even the way his head tilted–it all looked like Nicholas.

"Nicholas?" I whispered, my voice trembling with hope.

But as the light from the portal dimmed, my hope crumbled. The man wasn't Nicholas. His face was sharper, his clothes darker—black with silver chains, and strange symbols etched across his sleeves that pulsed with an otherworldly light. His eyes glowed an eerie shade I didn't recognize, and the aura around him felt colder. He stepped closer to me with a heavy black book clutched in his hands.

"Avery," he said, his voice resonating with a sense of urgency and despair. "There isn't much time."

I stared at him, bewildered and wary. "Who are you? What are you doing here?"

"My name is Benny," he replied, his gaze intense. "I'm sure this is hard to believe, but I am from the future. Nicholas's death and Adrian's rise to power set off a chain of events that will lead to a dark and terrible world. Adrian's plans extend far beyond what you can imagine. He aims to dominate the human race and subjugate all supernatural beings to his will."

My mind reeled with the implications of his words. "How can I stop him?"

Benny stepped closer, holding out the black book. "This book contains powerful spells—ancient, forbidden magic. You are the only one who can bring Nicholas back from Hell. He is the only one who can stop Adrian and his future plans. Without Nicholas, the future is lost."

I took the book, its weight and the dark energy emanating from it sending a shiver down my spine. "How do you know all of this?"

"In the future, Adrian's army will stop at nothing to ensure dominance," Benny explained, his voice growing more urgent. "They killed my wife, thousands of humans and supernatural beings alike. We can't let that future come to pass. Nicholas's return is our only hope."

My hands trembled as I held the book, the enormity of the task before me sinking in. "Bringing someone back from Hell...can that even be done?"

Benny nodded. "It can. It is dangerous and almost impossible, even for magic, but you must try. Time is running out. Adrian's influence is spreading, and soon it will be too late."

Before I could ask anything more, the portal began to close, the energy swirling faster. "Remember, Avery," Benny called out as he began to fade. "You are our last hope. Save Nicholas, save the future."

With that, he was gone, the portal sealing shut behind him. I was left alone in my room, the black magic book heavy in my hands and my heart pounding with a mix of fear and determination. The path ahead was fraught with danger, but I had no choice. I had to bring Nicholas back, for the sake of our world and the future that depended on it.

Avery

The next morning, I found Violet in the parlor, her face still marked with grief. I took a deep breath and sat down next to her, the black book clutched tightly in my hands.

"Violet, something happened last night," I began, my voice barely above a whisper.

She looked up at me, concern etched into her features. "What do you mean?"

"A man from the future visited me," I said, struggling to find the right words. "He brought this book. It contains spells—ancient, forbidden magic. He said I'm the only one who can bring Nicholas back from Hell, but that I must, to save the world."

Violet's eyes widened. "Avery, that sounds incredibly dangerous. Do you really think it's possible?"

I nodded, feeling the lingering connection to Nicholas pulsing faintly within me. "I have to try. Nicholas is the only one who can stop Adrian. Without him, our future is doomed."

Violet reached out and laced a hand through mine, hesitating. "I want to help you, Avery. But this is so risky. We need to consult the magical council. They might have the resources and knowledge we need."

Her words gave me a glimmer of hope. "You're right. We can't start a council and not get their insight, plus, we can't do this alone."

When we brought it to the council, the other supernatural beings listened intently as I explained Benny's visit and the importance of bringing Nicholas back. Despite their initial shock, they agreed to help. Each being offered their unique skills and knowledge to assist in gathering the necessary ingredients and preparing for the spell.

The werewolves, led by Marcus, helped me locate and dig up Nicholas's original bones. The task was grim, but Marcus's steady presence gave me the strength to see it through. We carefully transported the bones back, ensuring they were treated with the utmost respect.

On the night of the ritual, Violet and I stood by two large tubs filled with sacred water. One held Nicholas's bones, and the other was prepared for the spell. I took a deep breath, feeling the weight of the black magic book in my hands.

Violet squeezed my hand, her eyes filled with a mix of fear and determination. "Are you ready?"

I nodded. "We have to do this. For Nicholas. For our future."

The cool air prickled my skin, but I pushed aside my discomfort. Clutching the book, I stepped into the tub, feeling the sacred water envelop me,

As I began to recite the incantation, the room darkened, and a powerful energy swirled around us. The water in the tubs began to glow with an eerie light. I felt a pull, as if being drawn down into a hole.

Taking a deep breath, I lowered my whole body under the water, submerging completely. The sacred water closed over my head, and I felt the world shift around me.

Everything went dark.

When I rose, gasping for air, I found myself in Hell. The air was thick with heat and the smell of sulfur, and the ground beneath me was cracked and barren. I took a deep breath, steeling myself for the task ahead. I had to find Nicholas and bring him back, no matter the cost.

Acknowledgements

The following people/groups are only a snippet of the amazing team I have had behind me over the years.

To my mom: Thank you for loving me as I was and encouraging me to never stop using my imagination, even when it was dangerous.

To my husband: Thank you for listening to my thoughts and ideas, letting me bounce stuff off of you, and just never allowing me to give up. You truly are the best thing to ever happen to me. I love you.

To The Author Buddy: Thank you for helping me polish this book into the amazing story that it is become. Rachel, Perrin, and Jess thank you so much!

All Write Well: Thank you to the amazing group of people that taught me how become a published author!

To my readers: Thank you for giving my story a shot and living the adventure that has been in my head for years. I hope you enjoyed Nicholas's and Avery's love story!

About the author

Mystika is an oracle of the supernatural realm, gifted with the ability to perceive and record the intricate stories of magical beings. Her writing serves as a bridge between worlds, ensuring that these tales of wonder, power, and mystery are never forgotten. When she's not weaving the destines of the supernatural into captivating narratives, Mystika enjoys the enchantments of everyday life with her magical husband and their mischievous warlock toddler. Together, they create a world filled with love, magic, and stories that transcend time.

You can follow Mystika for future books and signings on Facebook HERE or Instagram HERE.